THEY CALL ME THE MERCENARY

#7

SLAVE OF THE WARMONGER

Books by Jerry Ahern

The Survivalist Series
#1: Total War
#2: The Nightmare Begins
#3: The Quest
#4: The Doomsayer
#5: The Web
#6: The Savage Horde
#7: The Prophet

The Defender Series
#1: The Battle Begins
#2: The Killing Wedge
#3: Out of Control
#4: Decision Time
#5: Entrapment

They Call Me the Mercenary Series
#1: The Killer Genesis
#2: The Slaughter Run
#3: Fourth Reich Death Squad
#4: The Opium Hunter
#5: Canadian Killing Ground
#6: Vengeance Army
#7: Slave of the Warmonger
#8: Assassin's Express
#9: The Terror Contract
#10: Bush Warfare
#11: Death Lust!
#12: Headshot!
#13: Naked Blade, Naked Gun
#14: The Siberian Alternative
#15: The Afghanistan Penetration
#16: China Bloodhunt
#17: Buckingham Blowout

THEY CALL ME THE MERCENARY

#7

SLAVE OF THE WARMONGER

JERRY AHERN

SPEAKING VOLUMES, LLC

NAPLES, FLORIDA

2012

THEY CALL ME THE MERCENARY

SLAVE OF THE WARMONGER #7

ISBN 978-1-61232-217-9

For Fran Hood—the woman Hank Frost could never forget, and for all the right reasons, too . . .

Chapter One

Hank Frost closed his eye, then opened it
again, turning his head back to look past the
pretty brown-haired woman seated on his left
beside the window. The ground seemed to
shrink below him. As he looked straight out the
window he could see long, thin clouds in the
distance at what seemed the edge of the bright
blueness of sky. There was a dinging sound and
he looked up, the "no smoking" sign winking
off. Frost fumbled in the pockets of his rumpled
blue suit for the half-empty pack of Camels and
his lighter, found them and fired one of the
cigarettes in the blue-yellow flame of his battered Zippo.

One hundred thousand dollars, he thought—
all of it in a Swiss account, just waiting for him.
That and a just-healing scar on his right arm
were what he had to show for the campaign in
Monte Azul where he led the forces of the ousted
anti-Communist government in recapturing

7

the strategically important Latin American nation. He let out a long breath.

In a way, the jungle fighting there had been easier than what he now faced. At least that was something he knew how to handle. For the first time in his life he had money. He wasn't rich, but one hundred thousand dollars was certainly serious.

But what to do about himself and Bess, he thought.

He looked down the aisle. There was some kind of activity near the forward cabin. He mentally dismissed it. It was a relatively short hop to Atlanta where he would layover for about a half-hour, then fly out to Albuquerque, New Mexico. An old friend from the security business owned a cabin in the mountains between Albuquerque and Santa Fe and had given Frost the option to use it as long as he wanted. Frost thought he might stay for a week, possibly two. It would be a good, quiet place to think.

There was a stewardess zig-zagging down the aisle. She was the pretty, model-type of stewardess with perfectly applied make-up, raven-dark hair and a professional smile that showed even white teeth. He watched the eyes though, and something was wrong there, the muscles around them tight, the eyes themselves glassy in their professional cheerfulness. It gave him a cold feeling in the pit of his stomach, and as the stewardess swished past him, the hem of the apron over her slacks brushing against the back of his hand, Frost snapped open his seat-belt, stubbing the Camel out in the armrest ash-tray. He glanced toward the rear of the cabin, saw the bathrooms and started unsteadily down the aisle, shifting his hands along the edges of the seatbacks. The ride was almost ground steady, he realized, but still something about walking in an amalgam of aluminum, steel, plastic and synthetic rubber thousands of feet in the air made it seem unsteady to him.

Frost reached the last row of seats and looked beyond them. On the portside of the plane was the galley and beyond that, one of the two aft bathrooms. He turned into the galley, leaning against the aluminum framework, his hand high over his head against the curtain rod. The stewardess, the one with the model's face, was unsuccessfully lighting a cigarette, her hands trembling. Frost reached out with his Zippo and held the flame in front of her. She seemed just to notice him then, he thought, and she forced the smile back onto her face and dipped her head forward, her hands still shaking as she cupped them around the fire in Frost's hand.

"What's the matter?" Frost asked, his voice in a whisper.

"The matter? Nothing—nothing's the—"

"This is the Captain speaking, ladies and gentlemen," the static-ridden intercom inter-rupted. Frost looked up at the speaker just inside the galley, as if he could read the face of the Captain there. "There is absolutely no reason to be alarmed—" Frost looked at the girl's face

"—but this flight is being diverted to Cuba." There was a shriek from someone up the aisle. "There are hijackers aboard, but I ask that you remain calm and stay in your seats. The hijackers have promised that if there is full cooperation, no one will be harmed. Recent experience with the Cuban government indicates we should be on the ground only long enough for refueling and then once again be on our way. Let me emphasize that there is no cause—" Frost stepped closer to the woman, forgetting about the Captain's voice as it droned on.

"If I go to Cuba, lady—I'm dead," Frost said flatly, his voice rasping in a whisper inches from her face. "Where are they and what have they got?"

"I don't—"

"Bullshit—you saw them, that's why your hands were shaking—are still shaking." Frost took the woman's hands in his own, steadying them. "Now tell me—and fast."

The professional smile on the woman's face seemed to crack. Frost decided they really were making mascara waterproof these days, because tears were streaming down the girl's cheeks as she leaned her head against his chest, but the eye makeup wasn't streaking. "Isabel—my friend. They've got a glass or plastic knife blade at her throat and threatened to kill her and slash anyone else they could if there was an attempt to stop them."

"Hmm," Frost smiled, tilting up the girl's

chin and looking into her eyes. "The old glass knife trick, eh?"

In spite of herself, the girl began to laugh. "Who are you? What—"

"See this eyepatch?" he asked her, leaning closer to her and whispering. "Well, it's really a disguise. Actually, I usually wear two eye-patches with slits in them to see out of them—and my white horse is on a later flight." The girl leaned against him, the sound of laughter mixed with the sniffing sound as she daubed at her face with a handkerchief. "That's better, kid," Frost told her. "Now—where are those suckers, so I know when the time comes."

"There—but, they might kill Isabel, or—," and she pointed up the aisle.

"I can't go to Cuba. Period. And they won't kill Isabel; I won't let them. Two guys?"

"Yes—I think that's all. By the small galley between First Class and Coach, they—"

"Anything else?"

"No—but, you—"

"Yes, I can," Frost said with more confidence than he actually felt. "Now, wipe your eyes and finish your cigarette. I'll move when I think it's time. Relax."

Frost turned and went into the bathroom, sliding the occupied sign into position, listening to, feeling the vibration of the aircraft tail section. He shrugged and raised the toilet seat and urinated, then flushed. He remembered once when he was a boy riding a train he had used the bathroom and had actually been able to look down through the trap in the bottom of the toilet and see the rails and ground below. He smiled at himself in the mirror—he was glad they didn't do that on airplanes. As he started to open the door, he stopped. He wondered if in the early days of aviation—"Naw," he grunted to himself.

Frost closed the door behind him and walked past the galley. The stewardess was still there, eyeing him, nervously he thought. But he noticed her hands weren't shaking anymore. He cocked his head to the left and gave her a wink with his right eye—one of the disadvantages of having one eye gone, he reflected. He walked up the aisle and sat down, beside the pretty brown-haired woman again. Frost reached in his pocket, opened the slim penknife blade on the moneyclip and started whittling at the buckle side of his seatbelt. The brown-haired woman looked at him. He looked at her brown eyes and smiled. "Hi!"

"What are you doing with your seatbelt?"

"Just nervous—gotta work with my hands. You know."

"No—I don't know. That's crazy!"

"What—cutting the seatbelt?"

"Yes."

"You're probably right—don't worry about it. I'm a stockholder in the airline."

"I don't believe that," the woman said.

"How about—I'm an airline safety inspector and this company has been reported to us for using cheap seatbelts?"

"I'm going to call—"

"Who—one of the hijackers?" Frost asked, looking at her.

"Then you tell me what you're doing—now!"

"I am fabricating a weapon."

"A what?"

"A mace or a flail—one of those medieval things. I could never remember which one was which. You know, swing it around, scream bloody murder and lace somebody across the puss with it. One of those."

"You're insane."

"Probably. So?"

"You're going after the hijackers—by yourself?"

"What—you volunteering?"

"No—but—"

"Then shut up—no offense."

"I will not! Why are you doing this?"

"You want to know the truth?"

"Well—yes, I do," she seemed to decide.

Frost shrugged, the knife blade almost through the tough seatbelt fabric. "I'm what people call a mercenary—at least sometimes. I just got back from Monte Azul. Ever hear of the place?"

"Isn't that the country that—?"

"Yep."

"You're the one-eyed man who led—"

"Yep. Right now, I figure I'd last about thirty seconds on Cuban soil before I got tossed in the nearest torture chamber or somebody did me a favor and put a bullet in me. I'd say between the eyes, but that'd be impossible," and Frost tugged at his eyepatch and smiled at her.

"You could get—the stewardesses, the passengers—"

"There's a stewardess up front with a knife at her throat. She could get killed. I don't think so, though—I'm waiting my chance. I'll create a diversion. You wanna help?"

"Of course I don't—you're crazy!"

"Yeah—well," and Frost finished whittling the belt from the seat and closed his little moneyclip knife. He wrapped the seatbelt one turn around his right fist, then gave the improvised weapon a trial swing to test the heft of the buckle. He wished it were heavier. Then Frost looked up.

A man was standing in the center of the aisle ahead, near the midcabin galley. "What the Captain say—he true. No body persons move or she is killed," and then Frost saw the second hijacker. The girl with the knife at her throat, her eyes wide, her face pale was evidently Isabel. A woman somewhere in the coach cabin screamed.

"Too many of the people get up, move around this aircraft I think—sit down. Every person."

Frost snarled at the hijacker under his breath, muttering, "Bite my ass."

"At first when a sign of trouble come, she will die and we will slit the throats of every passenger in the aircraft here." The hijacker was dark,

14

clean-shaven, dirty-shoed. He was about six feet tall, maybe one hundred-eighty pounds, Frost gauged. Frost didn't like the set of the man's neck—it was overly muscled, the sort of condition you get from wrestling or weight lifting. Frost looked up—the "no smoking" sign was on. He lit a cigarette anyway.

Frost looked at the brown-haired woman beside him. "What's your name?"

"Fran Hood. Why do you want to know?"

"Well, I'll tell you. Get up to go to the bathroom right now."

"Why should I?"

"'Cause if you don't, that girl up there is going to get her throat slit. Watch that second guy, the one holding her. He's as jumpy as a guy with colitis at a Mexican restaurant. Do as I say."

"I will not!"

"Come on, huh—please?" Frost smiled.

The girl started to shake her head, and Frost leaned closer to her. "How about I threaten you with bodily harm—hmmm? Just stand up and walk past me—period. Now!"

The brown-haired girl looked at him, her lips set in a cross between anger and frustration. "All right," she snapped.

The girl stood, then started past Frost, Frost swinging his legs a little into the aisle to let her pass. The hijacker shouted down the aisle, "Hey, woman, sit down!"

Fran Hood started back, and Frost reached his

15

right hand up under the hem of her dress and between her thighs and pinched.

She screamed, turned around and slapped at Frost's face, the hijacker shouting something Frost couldn't understand, but as Frost began to lean back in the seat to escape the girl's hands, he could see the hijacker starting toward them, three seat rows away. Frost pushed out with his right hand, shoving the girl named Fran across the aisle and into the lap of an old Chinese man. Frost's left hand was already moving up as he started out of his seat. The hijacker was less than a yard away, his hands reaching out, his mouth moving, cursing. Frost took the seatbelt flail and slapped it with his left fist across the hijacker's mouth. Frost turned his eye and face away as the hijacker's lips split and blood spurted all over the rear of the cabin.

Frost was on his feet then, his right knee smashing upward into the hijacker's crotch, doubling the man over. As Frost started past the man, he hooked his right fist low and hard into the side of the hijacker's head. There were men and women in the aisles, some of the women screaming as Frost pushed ahead past them.

"Georgio!" Frost thought it was the other hijacker's voice. "Georgio!"

Frost knocked a blonde-haired fat woman aside as gently as he could as he reached the forward cabin entrance. The second hijacker was standing there, his face white, his lips pale, his right hand shaking as he held the knife at the stewardess's throat. Frost stopped, glared at the man, then rasped, "Isabel—when I move, hit the deck." In the same instant Frost feigned right, and the hijacker twisted the woman around, moving the knife. Frost's left hand curved back and up and forward, the seatbelt flail in his fist. Frost's hand shot out as if to shield the woman as he grabbed for the hijacker's knife, the flail hammering down on the right side of the hijacker's head. There was a scream—from the hijacker—and the man started to stumble back, the stewardess half-falling, half being pulled by Frost's right hand, away from the knife.

Frost swung again with the flail, the hijacker half-crouched against the mid-cabin galley bulkhead. But as the flail crossed toward the hijacker's face, the man raked the transparent knife blade up and forward, the edge of the blade missing Frost's wrist, but the point hooking in the fleshy part of Frost's left hand and ripping open a gash. As the flail fell from his grip, Frost could already see his left hand streaming blood. Frost grabbed at the stewardess—Isabel—with his right hand, like a child playing crack the whip in a schoolyard, and snapped her body back down the aisle and behind him. His left hand hurt, badly, and he could feel the rawness of the gash as blood pumped from it, dripping onto the carpeted cabin floor.

Frost edged back a half-step, the hijacker on

17

his feet now, a wild-eyed look replacing the look of fear and indecision that had been there a moment earlier. The hijacker lunged like a streetfighter, his body low and in a crouch, the knife slashing ahead of him. Frost started moving back to avoid the knife, but stopped—there were passengers on both sides of the aisle and if he got between the rows of frightened and uselessly screaming people, each time the hijacker made a swipe with the knife, somebody would get cut.

Frost glanced to his right, his left, catching sight of a pillow on one of the seats. He reached out for it as the hijacker made the lunge, the knife blade crossing inches from Frost's face as the one-eyed man snapped his head and upper body back and away. But Frost had the pillow, crushing it in his left hand to both use as a shield of sorts and to stem the flow of blood from the cut.

"Come on—wimp!" Frost snarled, the hijacker backstepping, then half-diving, half-throwing himself forward. The knife blade punched outward toward Frost's throat. Frost dodged and crossed the hijacker's face with his right fist, missing the jaw but impacting on the nose, breaking it. Blood squirted from the hijacker's face, but the nose was broken sideways only. If he were going to connect with the nose, Frost thought, he wished he'd broken it front to back and been able to drive the bone up between the eyes and into the brain—an instant, fatal lobotomy.

Frost stumbled back, half-falling into the small galley. The hijacker wheeled and dived toward him with the knife. Frost started to react, then froze, the hijacker stopping as if in a single frame of movie film. The man's eyes were wide, then rolling upward. The hijacker's knees buckled, then he fell forward.

Frost rolled away, the hijacker crashing to the galley floor beside him.

Frost pulled himself up to his knees, snatching at the knife, prying the fingers of the hijacker's right hand from the taped handle. He stared at the instrument. It was clear plastic. Because there was no metal the hijacker had boarded the plane with it, right past airport security. Frost gingerly passed his thumb across the edge; it was as sharp as a piece of broken glass.

Frost, still on his knees beside the unconscious man, turned toward the galley entrance three feet away and looked up. "Thank you, Fran Hood," he smiled. It was the brown-haired girl he'd pinched on the thigh to start the whole diversion. In her right hand was a high-heeled shoe, the sole part clutched tightly in her fingers.

"I'm a nurse—let me see that hand," she commanded.

"Okay, but wait a minute." Frost climbed to his feet, looked down at the hijacker and kicked the man hard in the left side of the head with one of his sixty-five dollar shoes. The hijacker's body lurched up a little off the cabin floor from the impact.

"You kicked a man when he was down!" the brown-haired woman gasped.

Frost winked at her. "Only because it's easier that way."

Chapter Two

"I mean, I don't mean to sound critical, but weren't you awfully short with those policemen?"

Frost studied the drink in his hands, the left one heavily bandaged, then glanced down the mahogany-colored bar and back to the brown-haired woman beside him. "Awfully short with them? No—it's just that policemen are usually so tall, that's all."

The girl looked at him, then started to laugh. Frost decided he liked her brown eyes. "Are you ever serious?" she asked him.

"I try not to be," he admitted, then sipped at his drink.

"You know you shouldn't drink too much, maybe not at all with some types of antibiotics. You could—"

"You sure you've got to get to Atlanta tonight?" Frost interrupted, looking back at his drink.

"I just met you," she said, her voice soft, looking away.

"Yeah," Frost grunted, lighting a cigarette in the blue-yellow flame of his battered Zippo. "Like I said, though . . ." And Frost let the sentence hang.

"Yes—but look. Y'all have things to do, I've got a—"

"Can I see you sometime? Drive up to that town you live in—what's the name?"

"The town—it's—yeah, you can, I guess," she said, her voice still soft.

"That was a gutsy thing you did—whackin' that clown with the heel of your shoe."

"Well," she smiled. "I couldn't just stand there, like all those other people were doing—you know . . . I just kind of thought—"

"I know what you thought—you're a hell of a lady."

"Thank you," she smiled. Frost thought she looked embarrassed.

"But you're sure you've got to get back—tonight?"

"Yes—I'm sure," she told him, not looking sure at all, he thought.

"What are you going to do if sometime I drive up to that little house of yours and say, 'Here I am'?"

"I'll probably say, 'Hey, it's good to see you. Something like that, anyway." Clearing her throat, she asked, her voice different-sounding somehow, "What are you doing after you leave here?"

"I don't know," Frost told her. "The Feds want to see me tomorrow to wrap up their reports on the hijacking. Probably some hotshot lawyer will get hold of those two turkeys and figure out a way they can slap me with a lawsuit for punching them out. I don't know."

She glanced at her watch. It was black-faced, slightly larger than the average woman's watch; it reminded Frost she was a nurse. "I've got to catch my flight. Walk me to the gate?"

Frost looked at her, smiled and nodded, "Okay." He belted away the rest of his Seven & Seven and put some money down on the bar. They made small talk as they walked from the lounge area into the airport itself, stopping as Frost helped her verify her gate number on a closed-circuit television monitor. Yes, her luggage was aboard—no, she had to leave.

He passed through airport security with her, walking through the arch and getting stopped. "Stupid damn thing," he muttered, taking off his black-faced Omega Seamaster and handing it to one of the security cops. If the machines were calibrated improperly, the stainless steel of the case and the band sometimes set the metal detectors off. He was wanded, then passed through the archway again and this time nothing happened. As he put his watch back on, he saw the girl was waiting for him. He walked up beside her, then the two of them started toward her gate.

"Flight one-eleven Tri-Star service, Atlanta and New York City. Last call for boarding at gate—"

Frost interrupted the high-pitched, professional-sounding voice on the loudspeaker. "Look—what can I say!" he told the brown-haired girl.

"You don't have to say anything," she smiled.

"You're right," he smiled, stopping with her a few yards away from the boarding pass counter, standing there in the middle of the crowded corridor leading to the flight gates on all sides.

Frost reached with his left hand, noticed the bandages there and saw the girl's eyes. He moved his right hand then and touched it against her cheek, the tips of his fingers finding the hair at the nape of her neck. He watched her eyes. "I'm trying to remember—you'll say, 'Hey, it's good to see you.'"

"That's right—that's what I'll—"

Frost bent slightly down, his mouth touching her parted lips, kissing her, people jostling past them, feeling her responding against his lips. He looked at the brown eyes a moment, then with his good right hand held her hands. "Good-bye, Fran Hood." She smiled and Frost turned and walked away—he looked back once, and she was looking back too . . .

Frost turned down the corridor to the security office that was holding his luggage. Even if it hadn't been for the FBI and FAA and airline officials he had to see the following day, he would have had no desire to fly that night. His hand didn't really hurt; it was uncomfortable. But the knife fight aboard the plane had been a close thing. Frost stopped, a tiny alcove in the long, heavily trafficked corridor drawing his attention. There was a television set there—a big, color console, not like the small, black and white portable back at his seldom-used apartment in South Bend. But he saw his own face on the screen.

There was a small knot of people around the set and he jostled his way into a good spot. Brightly colored advertisements told of the high technology of the television set, its fine sound system—all of that. But the news broadcast talked about a one-eyed man foiling an airline hijacking. Frost smiled, his ego getting inflated. To the best of his knowledge, he'd never been on television before. He tried to catch the commentator's words.

". . . in what witnesses describe as a blood-chilling knife fight, Henry Frost singlehand-edly foiled a hijacking FBI officials say could have turned into a bloodbath. One of the hijackers—Georgio Calvera—was free on bond posted by relatives pending deportation hearings for alleged involvement in a string of armed robberies in the Miami area. The second hijacker—known only now as 'Cuchillo,' the Spanish word for knife—was already wanted by authorities as a suspect in a string of bizarre, fatal slashings in the state of—"

"Captain Frost?"

Frost turned around. The face was smiling, but the eyes weren't. Frost automatically looked down to the raincoat over the man's arm, the forearm at a right angle to the black, wavy-haired man's expensively tailored three-piece suit. Frost looked up into the eyes again. The face was tanned and Frost roughly judged him as Italian or Greek.

"That gun under the raincoat routine went out in the 1940s movies, fella," Frost rasped, turning back to look at the screen.

He could hear the man's whispered voice behind him, "Yeah—but it still works. You make one wrong move, you try to call out, any-thing—the gun goes off. Right?"

Frost looked at the man again, then started to laugh, but the laugh froze inside him. There were two other men a short distance behind the man with the raincoat, and the three men were as alike as volumes of an encyclopedia. "What do you want?" Frost started for a cigarette, watched the man with the raincoat tense, but reached into his pocket and lit the cigarette anyway. Lighting the Camel, Frost added, "Or let me guess. You say, 'You're comin' with us!' Right?"

"Shut up and—"

Frost looked at the man, then slowly, exhal-ing the gray smoke of the cigarette as he spoke, said, "You watch your mouth or whatever the hell you've got under that raincoat is gonna wind up gettin' planted where the sun never shines, asshole."

The man with the raincoat edged a half-step closer to Frost. Frost stood, not moving, his eye riveted to the man. "Your move," Frost snapped. "Go ahead—all these people, all these airport cops—and you'd better hope one slug nails me or you're gonna be too dead to get arrested. Come on—ruin your raincoat!"

The man's eyes flicked and Frost started to move, then heard a voice, "Albert—get lost. Take George and Stan with you—now."

Frost didn't take his eye off the man with the raincoat. The man turned his head to Frost's right and half-whispered, "But Mr. Sardi, we was—"

"Shut up," the voice said.

Frost looked at the man with the raincoat. "You heard him, Albert. Mr. Sardi wants you to shut up and get out. Go on, before I make you eat that raincoat."

The man tensed and started to move forward. Before Frost could finish the knee-smash he was starting as his bandaged left hand started toward the raincoat-covered gun, a man stepped between them. Frost stopped; so did the man with the raincoat.

"I said to leave and now, Albert." Then, as if Albert and his raincoat had ceased to exist, the man between Frost and the gunman turned around to face Frost. He stuck out a manicured hand, "I'm Phillip Sardi, Captain Frost. My client asked these gentlemen to convey his request for an informal, yet urgent meeting he'd like you to attend. Fortunately, he asked me to come along as well in case these gentlemen couldn't handle it."

"Fortunately for who?" Frost snapped. He wondered how long he could keep up the 1940s detective novel tough-guy routine and still keep a straight face.

"Whom, isn't it?"

"Yeah—come to think of it. Whom's your client, Mr. Sardi?"

"Very droll, Captain Frost. My client is a very important man, much in the press despite his best efforts to live a peaceful life. I'm sure a man such as yourself could appreciate that. I can't reveal his identity until we arrive at the meeting. But, there's one thousand dollars in it for you just to come—and more if you accept the proposition my client is prepared to offer."

"I can just imagine what your peaceful and unassuming client does for a living," Frost smiled. "No thanks. For once in my life, I can live without the thousand."

Frost started to turn away. He felt Phillip Sardi's hand on his arm. As Frost turned around, he figured he'd give the tough-guy routine one more shot. "You wanna keep that hand right there on the end of your wrist—or you wanna keep it in a formaldehyde jar on the bookcase?"

"You've made your point, Captain," Phillip Sardi remarked, moving his hand, then straightening the vest of his gray three-piece suit. "But perhaps I haven't made mine. If we could go somewhere to talk, I'd be most grateful."

"The bar?"

"That would be excellent."

Frost nodded, starting away from the crowd around the television set. The news broadcast was ending and he decided he'd missed watching the rest of the story about himself. There were several faces in the crowd, staring at him and at Sardi. Frost smiled, saying in a too-loud voice, "Just rehearsing for a play. Sounded believable, didn't it. A little-known work by William Shakespeare's obscure twin brother who became one of Elizabethan England's most noted chiropractors."

Starting after Sardi's back toward the bar, Frost decided some of the crowd had probably believed him.

Chapter Three

Sardi stopped at the entrance to the bar, but didn't go in. He turned instead, staring down at the floor a moment, then looking up at Frost. "My client is parked illegally, Captain. And there is a complete bar in the back of his limousine. We mean you absolutely no harm, and are not requesting your involvement in anything that even remotely violates good moral conduct. Please?"

Frost looked at the man, then slowly nodded. "Just keep your three pals out of my way. You carry a gun?"

"Of course not, sir!"

"Stay in front of me anyway. I'll walk out to the car, nothing more than that. I'll play it by ear from then on. Agreed?"

"You should recognize my client. You've met once before I understand."

"I don't get—"

The man—a lawyer, Frost assumed—smiled

enigmatically and started walking past the bar
and into the main airport lobby. Frost mentally
and physically shrugged and started after him.
They crossed the lobby and went through the
double automatic doors to the outside. The air
was warm despite the darkness of the night.
Frost reached up and pulled the black silk knit
tie he wore to half mast, glancing from side to
side as he sidestepped people racing to and from
flights. He could see the limousine—a pearl
gray Lincoln Continental Town Car with a
much-extended custom body, gray vinyl top,
television and telephone equipment and—he
could tell by the odd look under the artificial
lighting—bullet-proof glass, tinted a dark green
all around. The door opened as Sardi stopped
beside the limousine's passenger compartment
and Frost, still standing a good distance back
along the curb, bent low and peered inside. A
light—some kind of dome light apparently—
flicked on. In the passenger compartment, leaning forward, not smiling but somehow looking
expectant, was a face Frost had seen once before.
He didn't know the name, but he knew the occu-
pation. It was the older, paunchy man who
called a moment's truce at the shootout in the
main dining room at the upper New York state
Mafia conclave when Frost had gone there to
kill Roger Fairborne. Fairborne had set him up
with the drug warlords in Burma, nearly
causing him to be killed—or worse, crippled for
life. Frost had nailed his man, and as syndicate
bodyguards were moving in, this man—now

31

older and somehow wiser-looking—had intervened to let Frost get out of the room alive to prevent a bloodbath.

Frost stood motionless along the curb for a moment, watching the man in the back seat of the limousine watching him. He remembered the strong, tired-sounding voice, too, as the man under the dome light began, "Joseph Canaretti, Captain Frost. I did you a turn once, and now there's a favor I want to ask of you. I saw your face—that damned eyepatch—plastered all over the television news tonight and said, 'That's the man my boys been lookin' for for the last week.' Fortuitous, really. Could you get in and join me? My word nothin' will happen to you. Well?"

"Your word," Frost stated, his voice straight.

"Yes, my word. I don't want the FBI guys parked in that green car back there to get a parking ticket or nothin', so maybe we should hurry up, huh?"

Frost laughed, shook his head and walked toward the curbside back door of the limo. "Your word, huh?"

"Yes. Like the last time."

"All right," Frost said as he bent low and climbed into the car, plopping down on the leather seat beside Joseph Canaretti.

Sardi started in and looked at Canaretti. Canaretti nodded and Sardi instead extended his hand. "Captain Frost—a pleasure meeting you, sir. My three assistants will see that your luggage is retrieved if you'd like, and will ferry

32

it out to Mr. Canaretti's estate. If you wish, that is."

Frost looked at Canaretti, the older man saying, "You might wanna stay a while."

Frost shrugged, then found the luggage receipt and passed it across to Sardi. "My bags are with airport security. Maybe you'd better get 'em instead of our pals."

"A good suggestion, Captain. I'll be seeing you later then." Sardi shook Frost's right hand, smiled at Canaretti and stepped back out all the way to the curb, closing the door. In what seemed to Frost like less than a second, the limousine was moving, away from the curb and into the airport traffic.

Canaretti leaned forward, tapping on the glass partition. The glass slid open and Canaretti told the chauffeur, "Don't go too fast, Harry—don't want the FBI guys arrested for speeding or nothin'."

Then Canaretti leaned back, looked at Frost, and said, "Can I offer you a drink, Captain? I got Cutty, V.O., Boodles, Smirnoff—what's your poison?"

Frost nodded negative, saying, "I only drink if I'm driving—I like to be sober if somebody else is doing the wheelwork. What do you want, Mr. Canaretti?"

"I like that—you're direct, frank. You wouldn't think a man in my alleged business would say he admires honesty, but I do. That's why I wasn't too upset you whacked that schmuck Fairborne up in the mountains there.

He wasn't honest."

"So then what do you want?" Frost persisted.

"You look like you could use a good meal. I'm takin' you to dinner at my place on the beach. I'll tell you all about it over dinner. I got a great cook. You like Italian food, Frost?"

"Yeah, I like Italian food. Why can't you tell me now?"

"Captain, you should realize more than most men that gentlemen don't—how should I put it—express themselves. I am not a salesman. I'm not hustling you on something, and I'm not even taking you for a ride like they say in the old movies—you know?"

Frost nodded that he knew.

"I'm a businessman—legitimate is how you interpret it. This is a matter both of business and of family—and not the kind of family you think either. And because of that it requires that we sit like men and talk and discuss."

"I'm not knockin' anybody off for you, Canaretti," Frost inserted.

"I'm offended you'd think I'd ask you that. Although there may be some violence involved in my proposal. But we can discuss that— dinner is the time. And would you reconsider the drink?"

Frost shrugged. "V.O.—please."

"I may take a little myself," Canaretti nodded. As he pushed the button beside him there was a mechanical sound and a bar unfolded out of the back of the front seat. Canaretti observed, "I really been lookin' for you for a week—nobody else would do. You know, I got a lot of talent available to me. I tried some of it—didn't do shit, Frost. A friend who works for one of the news programs called that he'd seen you in the tape being edited for the program on the hijacking. You are a brave man. I read your service record, too. Checked you out with Diablo security, the whole ball of wax. You're a good man. How'd you lose the eye, anyway—if it isn't too personal a matter for you?"

"Well, not much of a story really," Frost began, smiling. "See, I was stranded on this desert island once with this beautiful girl—I liked her to pluck grapes into my mouth, just like in the movies. Well, this one day, she was pulling the grapes out of the bowl beside my head there on the sand, plucking them into my mouth, nice as you please. I'd thought there was somethin' peculiar about her ever since I met her. Well, little did I realize—let me tell you. She was reachin' for another grape and—well, she had really long nails." Frost shook as if shuddering, then tugged at his eyepatch. "I didn't realize she was nearsighted. What an experience. Needless to say, I spit it right out, but by then, well—"

"I like a man with a sense of humor in these difficult times, Captain. I really do, you know," and Canaretti handed Frost a glass half-filled with amber liquid. "Grapes—son of a—" and Canaretti started to laugh.

Chapter Four

Frost stood under the cold water for several minutes, his body and his hair washed and rinsed, the cold water somehow reviving him. After several minutes when the water no longer seemed cold at all, Frost shut the shower head, pushed back the glass door and stepped out onto the bath mat. He'd shaved, brushed and flossed his teeth and now, toweling dry, he strode naked across the floor out of the bathroom. In the bedroom, he rummaged through his suitcase, finding a fresh pair of underpants, a pair of dark socks and a white shirt, then took his clean but rumpled white suit from the suit bag and started to dress. He stood in front of the mirror, staring at the scar where his left eye had been, shook his head disgustedly at himself, then took a fresh eyepatch and put it in place. He crumpled the paper that had covered the patch and discarded it in the wastebasket beside the dresser. He combed his dark brown hair, and in the strong light noticed the gray there—it was starting to catch up to his sideburns and his chest. The mustache, though, for some peculiar reason Frost couldn't fathom, seemed unchanging. It was still a dark, almost reddish brown. It needed a trim but he wasn't in the mood. He knotted the black tie in place instead. He'd just picked up a new Alessi shoulder rig for the Browning High Power and tried the leather harness across his back. He stripped it off, adjusted the coupler in the center for a little extra room, then tightened the rear strap on the gunside of the harness to elevate the muzzle portion of the holster and drop the butt lower. He tried it, this time with the Metalifed Browning High Power in place, checking it in the mirror. He stripped the holster and harness from his body once again, securing the harness with the Chicago-style screws now that he had it properly adjusted, then slipped the rig back in place.

Standing in front of the mirror, he reached up, ripping the High Power from the leather as soon as his right fist locked around the black rubber Pachmayr grips. He stared at himself in the mirror, then started to laugh, muttering, "Bang-bang." He shook his head as he reholstered the gun. He began the short but fruitful search for his Gerber knife—an original Mk I— and secured the knife inside his trouser band on the right side. Frost found his cigarettes, his money clip, everything he usually carried in his pockets and then slipped on the jacket of the white suit. He studied himself in the mirror, not out of vanity, he thought, but out of necessity. The gun didn't show; he liked that about Alessi rigs, having used them often before. They fit well and concealed the gun. Frost snatched up his Omega and locked it around his wrist as he started out of the room, not bothering to lock his door, lighting a cigarette with the Zippo as he walked to the edge of the banistered landing and gazed down onto the first floor below.

There was a maid moving about, doing something with a tray with wine glasses on it. He could smell something from the direction of the kitchen and the smell made him eager to find out what exactly it was. He shrugged, then started down the semi-circular staircase toward the checkerboard black and white tile first floor.

Canaretti had said he'd be waiting on the veranda. Frost aimed himself in what he hoped was the proper direction and started walking. He stopped before sliding glass doors, edged one open and could smell the sea, hear it. At what seemed to be the other end of a garden and down several low stone steps he could see a table and part of Canaretti's bulk outlined by it. "Must be the veranda," Frost murmured, then walked through the glass doors, between the rows of plants and down the steps toward the table. As he reached the bottom of the steps, he stopped. He could see the elaborate table setting. Beyond it was a low railing and beyond that a beach, gleaming almost white under the moonlight, with the dark, brighter white-edged breakers rolling from the almost impenetrable blackness beyond.

"Mr. Canaretti," Frost said, stopping slightly behind the man. "You've got a beautiful place. It restores my faith in ill-gotten gains and everything."

Canaretti looked up and around, smiled and shook his head, "So, you think that you can make a moral judgement on me—'ill-gotten gains.' What's ill-gotten, running a supermarket and hiking the prices fifteen percent the day before a ten-percent-off sale? Fixin' somebody's car and using old parts you scarfed off another heap and then chargin' for new? That's okay, huh?"

Frost shrugged, "Maybe you got a point. Where do you want me to sit?"

"Right beside me. You can see the water, and we can see each other's faces as we talk. I read your face the first time I saw you, a tough guy, a smart ass, everything I like. You remind me of myself when I was your age."

"Thanks?" Frost asked, raising his right eyebrow quizzically.

"Yeah—thanks!"

Frost sat down, stubbed out his cigarette in the ashtray beside his place setting and almost immediately there was a white jacket-clad young man at the table, replacing the ashtray with a fresh one. The young man returned, pouring a glass of wine from a large carafe. Frost sipped at it—it was red, fruity-tasting—he didn't know what it was. "This like Sangria?"

"Yeah, sorta. You like it?"

39

"Yeah—sorta," Frost told Canaretti.

"Good. We'll eat in just a sec here. We've got another guest for dinner. Be down in a little bit. I guess. Drink more wine—unless it gets you whacked. You'll need to think clear tonight. I'm gonna need a decision right away after you get the dope—that's the wrong word, isn't it? The information, let's say, huh?"

Frost smiled, but as he lit another cigarette and took a healthier swallow of the wine, he decided he was getting irritated with the folksy side of a Mafia Capo's home life. "Why don't you just tell me, Mr. Canaretti, hmm? I mean all it is is a yes or no you want, right? So, tell me and I'll give you one—a yes or no."

"Yeah, but it's a long story. You need the whole picture."

"Mr. Canaretti," Frost began, thoughtfully, staring at the wine glass, almost afraid to put out his cigarette because the white-jacketed young man would come back and replace the ashtray. "Is this business of yours like they portray it in the movies—I mean, the offer you plan to make. What happens if I say no?"

"You mean like that one movie there was? If you say no, I'll be crushed. But you won't be. Okay?"

Frost decided he didn't believe Canaretti—and he didn't think Canaretti thought he did. Frost stubbed out his Camel and started to say as much, then stopped.

"Hey—Julie," Canaretti enthused, standing.

Frost stood up as well. Standing at the top of

the low stone steps was a raven-haired, tall, dark-eyed woman. She had high cheekbones, tasteful and expensive-looking jewelry, almost bare shoulders, and an ankle-length white dress. Like the woman herself, everything about her seemed expensive, precisely designed and perfect.

The woman—Julie, Canaretti had called her—smiled warmly, lifted the skirt of her dress a little with the manicured thumb and first finger of her left hand, then started down the steps. She stopped, standing midway between Frost and Canaretti, Canaretti saying, "You look like ten million bucks, Julie. This is Captain Hank Frost. Frost," and Canaretti smiled as he gestured toward the woman, "This is Julie Pulman. You probably read about her in the fish wrappers, huh?" Frost and the woman touched their hands together. Canaretti laughed, edging back from his chair, the white-coated young man—Frost decided the guy would be called a steward—tugging out the chair on Canaretti's right, just opposite Frost, holding it until Julie Pulman sat down.

"So you are the man Mr. Canaretti's been searching for. I've read your vital statistics, Captain Frost. It sounds like you're right for the job."

Despite the incredibly beautiful woman opposite him, Frost decided he'd had enough. "What job, Miss Pulman? I read about you. Some woman's magazine about a year ago. I was waiting to get my teeth cleaned at the dentist's office. Worked your way through college as a high fashion model, one of the top paid women in the business, then quit when you graduated and became a police officer. Stayed with the cops for—what was it?"

"Eighteen months, Captain Frost," Julie Pulman interjected.

"Right—then started your own private investigations and security firm. Used the contacts from the modelling business to get big clients. You specialize in missing persons—missing rich persons, right? People who can afford big bucks to get jobs done the police can't do. I read you were on retainer with a lot of big corporations for executive protection—"

"Just like Andrew Deacon's Diablo Protective Services, right?" The girl smiled, lighting a cigarette for herself with a Dunhill lighter.

"Yeah, only more bucks. So—" Frost lit a cigarette for himself, almost tempted to slap the hand of the white-jacketed steward as he exchanged ashtrays—"who got kidnapped?" Frost turned and looked at Canaretti.

Canaretti said nothing a moment. Frost eyed the girl then—she stared at the glass of wine the white-coated steward poured. Finally, in an oddly choked-sounding voice, Canaretti said, "The guy here—he's deaf and he doesn't lip read. Valuable man to have around. We can speak freely. It's my—my daughter, Frost. You're a smart one—I wondered if you'd figure it."

"You've got your own soldiers, Mr. Canaretti—if she's—"

Canaretti hammered his fist down on the table, spilling his wine glass, the steward almost jumping to it and starting to mop it up. The placid look, the smiling, the benign old man routine—they were all gone.

"Do you want me to tell him, Mr. Canaretti?" Julie Pulman asked, her voice, too, odd-sounding.

"Tell me what? Somebody's been kidnapped. You hired her, and she needs military-type backup. Count me out. Your lawyer said nothing—"

"Frost," Canaretti began. "It's got nothin' to do with my alleged business, nothin' to do with somebody puttin' the muscle on me through somebody else. It's my daughter—Jesus!"

"Let me explain, Captain," Julie Pulman began, stubbing out her cigarette, the deaf steward replacing the ashtray almost immediately, Canaretti's wine already miraculously replaced, a linen napkin covering the portion of the table where it had spilled. Frost shook his head.

"Captain?"

"Yes," Frost responded.

"What do you know about white slavery?"

"What do you mean?"

"I mean," she persisted, "you know what white slavery is? Right?"

"Yeah—but what's that—" Then Frost shut up, turned and looked at Canaretti and despite the hovering steward, Frost lit a cigarette—he'd risk a new ashtray.

"My daughter," Canaretti said, his voice tired and old-sounding. "Some bastards put the bag on her, white slavers. I tried, my lawyers, my people—we can't get her out."

"Why not?" Frost asked.

"Tell him—I can't," Canaretti said, turning to Julie Pulman, then staring down at his empty hands.

"So tell me," Frost said, looking at the girl.

"Louise Canaretti, age twenty-five, Mr. Canaretti's only surviving child," and Julie Pulman emphasized the word "surviving."

"My son, Bob—was killed five years ago—with this thing," and Canaretti gestured to the air.

"Your alleged business?" Frost asked.

Canaretti nodded, saying nothing more.

"Louise Canaretti is brilliant," Julie Pulman went on. "She'd recently completed all her course work in postgraduate paleontology. She so distinguished herself that while she was working on her doctoral dissertation she was invited to participate in a very much publicized fossil hunt—you'd call it that, I guess—in the Middle East, near the border with Akaran. She disappeared, leaving all her things in her room. There was no ransom note—nothing. Mr. Canaretti called me. I had much the same sort of built-in pre-prejudices you have. But this has nothing to do with Mr. Canaretti's reputation. It could have happened to any girl—almost any. She would have had to be pretty, like Louise

44

Canaretti. It took me four days before I pieced together what happened."

"And what happened?" Frost asked, lighting another cigarette, by now resigned to the steward's ashtray fetish.

"She was kidnapped by a local unit of a widespread white slavery gang operating in the Middle East and southern Europe. They take customer orders, then go out and steal someone to specifications."

"Just like that?" Frost said, surprised.

"Just like that—like ordering a car with a special list of options. Their biggest customer is the Sheik of Akaran. Various American and European girls have been spotted over the years in his harem. Most of the women kidnapped by the white slavers are American girls, Germans, some French, some Italian, every once in a while an Englishwoman. I researched it and Louise fits the Sheik's regular order profile and rumor has it his harem just had a recent addition."

"What about the State Department?"

"Not a thing they can do, Frost. They already sent a diplomatic note. The Sheik is militantly anti-American. He never responded to the note, except to say he didn't know what the State Department was talking about, period. The State Department can't go any further because he's tied in with pro-American Arab groups and muscling him could cause too many problems. And that bastard knows it. So he sits there and laughs. Meanwhile, the Canaretti girl is his slave. As long as she pleases him, fine. But a friend in Israeli intelligence tells me the Sheik has a reputation with his women. Once they displease him, he turns them over to his guards. They do what they want with the girl, then he has her executed—usually in some painful way. Most of the girls co-operate, try to make him feel like some sort of god or something. It's the only way to stay alive."

"I'll kill the—"

"Mr. Canaretti—please," Julie Pulman implored. "That wouldn't do any good. But the fact remains, Captain Frost, that Louise Canaretti is Mr. Canaretti's daughter—in more ways than one. I wanted to know what kind of a person I was looking for. Too often investigators so much concentrate on the kidnappers, they forget obvious clues in the personality of the victim. In Miss Canaretti's case, she had a reputation for forthrightness, strength of character—toughness we might call it. I can't see her lasting too long with the Sheik. I think she would have been smart enough to play along as the only thing she could do as a means of staying alive, biding her time. But if she tries to escape, he'll kill her. If she loses her temper and the Sheik realizes her plan, he'll kill her. If she withholds herself from him, he'll kill her. I think she's still alive, but for how long I don't know. If Mr. Canaretti hadn't found you, I would have gone there myself within another two days."

"I can't see," Canaretti said softly, "can't see

Louise puttin' up with no crap no matter what some friggin' camel jockey tells her he's gonna do."

"What do you want from me?" Frost asked both of them.

"I need a different kind of soldier than my own people," Canaretti began. "My boys, you put 'em down in a desert, they'd get lost with no street signs. They don't know beans about commando stuff. I had you looked up after that thing in upstate New York. If there was one thing I figured about you—especially after that deal that went down in Burma—it was you never give up, even when you should give up. Am I right? Huh?"

Frost thought a moment. Actually, he reflected, Canaretti had made a pretty incisive character analysis. I am stubborn, Frost realized.

"I needed somebody now who could come through when the chips were down—a tough man, somebody who would not give up on me and say it was too hard, too dangerous."

Frost, no hint of humor in his voice, said, "That's an apt description of a fool, Mr. Canaretti."

"Frost," and Canaretti leaned forward, slowly beginning to speak, his eyes darting away from, then settling—rock steady—on Frost. "In my alleged profession, I'm alleged to be head of something the press calls the Five Families in New York, and I'm also alleged to be the head of something called 'Il Commissione,' whatever

47

the hell that is. I'll pay you any reasonable or unreasonable sum to get my daughter out of this and help Julie Pulman. If you don't help me, well . . ." Canaretti made an expansive gesture with his hands. "I would take it very personally. I realize I can't expect a man who doesn't know me to risk his life for my daughter. But perhaps someday you'll have a need for some help—I don't know. Who knows what the future will bring to any of us? You can be sitting here, like you are, one minute, healthy, a whole lot nearer to being young than I am, full of life—then poof! But my loyalty to friends who help me in a time of need is without bounds."

"I wouldn't want to feel you were threatening me," Frost smiled, looking at Canaretti.

"How can I threaten a man to make him risk his life? No, you can walk away. I said that, I meant that. But I don't read it in you that you could walk away from something like this. About money—anything you want and you know that. But more, I think you're what the kids—I got grandnieces and nephews—what they call a good guy, right? Well, we need a good guy. My bad guys, if they could really be called that, my guys, well, they can't do it. What do you say?"

"My fee, money for the people I'll need, expenses—"

"Yeah," Canaretti nodded.

"Yeah," Frost nodded back, thinking he sometimes amazed himself with his own stupidity.

Chapter Five

"I didn't think you'd do it, Captain Frost,"
Julie Pulman said, stopping by the stone sea
wall on the boundary line of the beach. She
leaned against it and pulled off her shoes.
"Can't walk in the sand with these," she added.
Frost looked at her as she removed the silvery-
colored, high-heeled shoes.

"Here—give 'em to me," Frost told her,
taking the shoes and sticking one in each outside pocket of his suitcoat.

"You are a funny man, Frost."

"Call me Hank," he told her.

"All right. You are a funny man—Hank. I
didn't think you'd do this deal for him."

"Why are you doing it?" Frost asked her.

"It's my kind of job, really. I specialize in kid-
nappings, missing persons, crimes against the
wealthy and the famous—all of that. But why
should you do this?"

"Money," Frost shrugged, watching his sixty-five dollar shoes sinking in the sand as he walked beside the girl, paralleling the surf as they gradually increased the distance between them and the house.

"What? You asked for a quarter-million dollars. You could have gotten four times that."

"I'm gullible," Frost smiled.

"I was waiting for you to ask for magic beans or something," the girl laughed.

"You remind me of someone," Frost confided, impulsively, instinctively, reaching out, taking the woman's hand. The hand stiffened in his and they both stopped walking, his eye meeting her eyes.

"What are you doing?" Julie Pulman asked, her voice low.

"Starting something, maybe," Frost told her.

"Who do I remind you of—you the kind of guy who carries a torch?"

"You're a mind reader," Frost told her.

"What—you think eye patches are a turn-on?"

"Different strokes," Frost smiled.

"Just what are you starting?" the girl asked, but didn't wait for an answer. She slipped her hand from his, then walked along down by the surf. The waves washed up toward her and he watched as her left hand caught at her skirt, hitching it up away from the water. Frost stepped out of his sixty-five dollar shoes, stocking-footed starting after her.

"Julie—"

"What, Hank?"

"I, ahh—"

"I know. You want to know the plan. Well—"

Frost walked down toward her, stopping a few feet away. He couldn't put his own shoes in his pockets; they were already crowded with her shoes.

"The plan—hmm. Well, I'll accompany your team. When you make the penetration, I'll be right there—"

"I was counting on that," Frost told her. "The penetration part, I mean."

"Do you want to go for a swim—now?"

"You first," Frost told her, then watched as the girl started back up away from the surf. She set her handbag down in the sand, then reached back—provacatively Frost thought—unzipped her dress, shrugged her shoulders forward and let it drop down, then stepped out of it. It was a warm night, he reasoned—the girl wore nothing under the dress except a small, strapless bra and a pair of lace-trimmed panties. She dropped the dress on top of the bag and started running toward the surf. Frost stripped away his jacket, his shoulder holster and knife, his tie. He watched the girl. "The hell with it," he rasped, unbuttoning his shirt as he ran down into the surf after the girl, throwing the shirt onto the sand, diving into the water after her.

A wave broke over his head and Frost pushed up from it. Seeing the girl, he reached out, grabbing at her cold, wet arms, pulling her close to him. "You're still wearing your pants," she smiled, almost giggling.

"It's wash and wear—this is a test," he told her, pulling her closer to him, the surf smashing against them, working around their legs and bodies and almost seeming to suck them down. Frost's right hand moved along the girl's body, stopping on her left breast, the nipple erect through the fabric of the strapless white bra under the palm of his hand.

"Just what are you doing—Captain Hank Frost?"

"I'll tell you as we go along," Frost smiled, drawing the girl against him, feeling the conflicting wet and cold and the heat of her body against his chest as he lowered his face toward her, kissing her, the lips wet, salty-tasting from the water, warm as they moved against his mouth.

He walked her out to the sand, pulling her down as he dropped to his knees, stripping away his pants. She did something he didn't see with the bra, and it whisked away, the panties all that remained. He stripped away his own underpants. "Your turn," he told her.

"I'll get sand—"

"We can wash it off," Frost reminded her.

"I don't usually kiss on the first date."

"How about heavy petting?"

"Only occasionally," she smiled.

"Is this to clinch the deal?" Frost asked her candidly.

"Let's just say it's a clinch."

"Let's say that," Frost said, pulling the girl toward him, both of them still on their knees.

His left hand reached down and ripped the panties away from her. She screamed a little, biting into his right ear as she did. Frost pushed her back. He was on top of her, the wet clothes were under them, and the surf was lapping against the soles of his feet, making him cold there while he was otherwise now warm as he held her, explored her, moved against and into her.

"Your heavy petting—I can—"

Frost crushed his mouth down on hers, then feeling her, hearing her breathing hard in his ear, he whispered, "Sometimes the only way to make a dame shut up is to kiss her."

"What—1940s—movies—ohh, Hank—movie did that line come—from, ohh," she moaned.

"You talk too much," Frost told her, then did something about it . . .

The water in the shower in Frost's room was warm—to both Frost and the girl. The water streaked down on them from the shower head, both of them soaking under it. He soaped her back, and she soaped his chest, washing each other as they talked, loudly over the spray of the shower. "So what's your plan, kid?" Frost asked her.

"The only one I could think of—you're not going to like it. But then neither do I really. There just isn't any choice really, you know?"

"I can't know until you tell me," Frost reminded her, washing her left shoulder, step-

53

ping back a half-step and almost slipping as she started to wash his genitals.

"You like that, huh? One-eyed men and two-eyed men—they're all the same," the girl laughed.

"You wash men a lot, huh?"

"Heavens no," she laughed. "Anyway, I got a lot of information on what the Sheik's personal-wants profile is. He likes girls about my height," she said, breathless as Frost washed her abdomen and below it. She leaned against him, kissing him on his mouth as the shower sprayed down on them. "He likes girls my height—blondes generally, but I can fix that. I wasn't a model for nothing. You learn a lot about makeup and who does the best jobs. I can get my hair dyed."

"Down there too?" Hank asked, and the girl screamed a little.

"Yes—there too."

"A real blonde—huh kid?" Frost rasped, faking a movie-sounding voice.

"Yes," the girl laughed. "A real blonde. But anyway, I set myself up to get snatched by the white slavers, while you and your team follow. I make myself the inside man—so to speak—get you out the poop you need, then you guys come in like D-Day and rescue the Canaretti girl and spring me. We'll shoot our way out if we have to, but hopefully we won't—we could run the risk of losing the girl that way. Then we boogie home. Simple as one-two-three."

54

"You're an idiot. You could get killed or worse."

"It's the 'or worse' part that worries me. But, unless you've got something better, that's the way we do it, Hank. And, if that doesn't work— say the white slavers are all on vacation—or they just don't grab me, then we think of something else. I'm open to suggestion."

"Why don't you just commit suicide then? It's easier and you could save the air fare for the body on the return trip," Frost remarked, holding her in his arms under the hot water.

"I've taken chances before—I'm a big girl."

"Well," Frost said, kissing her, then looking at her under the water in his arms. "You're right about that last part anyway."

Chapter Six

Using Canaretti's house as base of operations and running up a telephone bill Frost didn't even want to consider, well before breakfast he was already confident of securing two of the six mercenary soldiers he'd determined best for the operation. He'd even awakened one of the men, Aaron Cohn, in California at four a.m. The most important man to the operation, as Frost envisioned it, was Maurice Gilder. Gilder was a black mercenary and veteran of numerous African campaigns. He'd spent several months in Akaran once on a security assignment before the Sheik had assumed power from his dead, very pro-American father. And Gilder fluently spoke Farsi, the native language of Akaran. When Gilder wasn't doing a mercenary job, he spent his time writing language texts and serving as a language instruction and translation consultant for a prominent language school in Paris.

It took Frost eighteen telephone calls to track down Gilder's current location. He was staying in Norway having completed work on a language text that involved a detailed study of the Lapps.

By lunchtime, Frost had reached his sixth man, Caldwell Miles. Miles' most distinguished talent was that he had trained for three years with Japan's most distinguished Ninja master. Between mercenary assignments, Miles worked as a Hollywood stuntman, specializing in anything that involved martial arts work or wall or mountain climbing. He once climbed the side of a fifteen-story building completely without mechanical aid for an action/adventure film.

Frost tore a bite from a sandwich Julie Pulman had brought to him on the veranda—hot pastrami on an onion roll—and watched as the girl leafed through his notes. "No respect for privacy you got," Frost laughed.

"You've got some good people—like this guy Gilder, and this Miles man. I didn't realize men that talented worked as mercenaries. I always had the idea most mercs were losers—no offense."

"Ohh," Frost began through a mouth of sandwich, "hell—none taken—uh-uh."

"You know—this Gilder—I've read his stuff. Miles—I saw him interviewed on television once—I've seen his stunts. Aaron Cohn—hell. I worked with Aaron once years back. He's a security specialist. All of them mercenaries?"

"It depends on what you call a mercenary, really," Frost told her, looking out toward the ocean, feeling a breeze blowing up from the surf. "This isn't anything weird or strange, this job. It's the kind of thing half the guys in the United States would do for free. I mean," and Frost took a swallow of Michelob to wash down part of the sandwich, "there's some American girl, kidnapped by some foreign creep who wants to violate her virtue and all. To top it off, the guy's known to be anti-American and anti-Israeli. He's a creep. Save some American girl from dishonor at the hands of some foreign anti-American creep. Hell," Frost laughed, "if I let word of this leak to the newspapers, we could field an army of ten thousand guys against the Sheik of Akaran, Ali Hassan Foudani. We could make Akaran look like a wet spot in the sand. Lots of people these days aren't happy with two-bit tin-plated dictators in the Middle East. Are you?"

"No—I guess you're right." The girl lit a cigarette in the wind—Frost mentally chalked up five points for her—then sat down opposite him. She was wearing white shorts, sandals, and one of those tops, Frost thought, that stayed up by friction. There weren't any straps holding it to her neck or shoulders, and there was nothing much below where it covered her breasts either. "My people in the area around Akaran gave me a report about an hour ago. As far as they can ascertain, the white slavery gang is still in operation, and still looking for possibles."

"What happens if those guys put the bag on you and plan to sell you to somebody else— maybe the potentate of Pittsburgh instead of the Sheik of Akaran?"

"No big deal, Hank. You and your guys will rescue me. It's a cinch."

"I never asked you," Frost began, finishing the last of his sandwich and washing it down with beer, "but how many guys are there in this white slaver gang—just in case it comes to a fight with them?"

"Forty in the Akaran area, give or take a half-dozen. Why?"

"Forty? Oh," and Frost stared out to sea. There was Gilder, Miles, Cohn, Luciano, Bohls and Smith, all of them good, with guns and with anything else. There would be arms waiting for them when they arrived in North Africa, all the equipment they'd need. Six mercenaries, plus himself, plus the girl. She was pretty good with weapons so far as Frost knew. Eight people. Frost started laughing.

"What's so funny, Hank?" Julie Pulman asked, leaning toward him.

Frost caught a glimpse of her cleavage, then lit a cigarette in the blue-yellow flame of his Zippo. "Eight of us," Frost began, "eight against forty or so white slavers and the Sheik of Akaran's army. We shouldn't take advantage of those guys like that. Ohh," and Frost just shook his head. The girl had been right—he should have asked for more money.

Chapter Seven

Separate arrivals had gotten Frost and Julie Pulman into North Africa. As he walked beside Julie through the dusty town square, Frost still hardly recognized her. Her hair was dyed so perfectly blonde that the previous night, despite a detailed search that had started Julie Pulman laughing so uncontrollably they'd almost awakened the entire hotel, Frost had found not even a single dark root—anywhere. There had been no time to arrange to get weapons legally out of the U.S. and into the Middle East, but Julie Pulman had covered that nicely, too. She'd once saved the son of one of Greece's most powerful gun runners and one of his local "salesmen" was waiting now in the small town of Bharanabad with the tools Frost and his people would need.

As they reached the far side of the square, Frost pushed up his dark glasses and peered at the doorway, then glanced back to Julie Pulman. She, like Frost, was dressed as a tourist, both of them festooned with camera and lens cases. Frost wore an open collar white short-sleeved shirt and tropical weight slacks, and Julie wore a pale blue top, a khaki skirt and sandals. Both wore sun glasses.

Frost knocked again on the rough, weathered wooden door and finally heard a voice from inside, "Who is there?"

"Sam and Suzie Schmulowitz from San Sabastien," Frost responded, feeling stupid, hearing Julie Pulman almost laugh out loud. Frost looked at her, "Well, you said the guy needed code names. It was the best I could come up with before we left." As Frost started to turn back toward the doorway, the door opened. A man looking for all the world like a character actor who'd taken the wrong turn stood framed in the doorway. He wore a white suit, a red fez and was no taller than five foot six.

"Ahh, the lovely couple, yes," the fez-clad man smiled.

"Yes," Frost muttered, then half-pushed past the man as he guided Julie Pulman through the doorway and inside the small, cool, bare struc-ture. It was a warehouse, perhaps for rugs, Frost thought, judging from the long poles aban-doned all over the floor. On the far side of the building were double, garage-type doors, these also of wood. Parked just inside them was a dusty, white International Travelall.

"The things you expressed interest in are this way." The man with the fez, wringing his hands together, smiled.

Frost started across the building floor. He stopped behind the vehicle, opened the rear deck and inside saw several prayer-sized Oriental rugs. He looked over his shoulder as Julie and the man with the fez who worked for the Greek gunrunner approached. "These are nice rugs," Frost commented.

"Under the rugs you shall find what you like," the man remarked.

Frost rolled back one, then all of the rugs. There was a large crate and, the Pulman girl helping him, they moved back the lid. "Where the hell did you get these?" Frost asked, turning and looking at the man with the fez, then looking back into the crate. The long guns were brand new M16A1s, marked as U.S. Government Property, and there were various handguns—these, too, obviously U.S. Government property at one time, and all brand new— 1911A1 .45 automatics and Smith & Wesson Combat Masterpiece .38 Specials. There was a shorter, taller box beside the crate containing the guns and Frost opened this to find boxes of .38 Special full metal-jacketed military ball ammo, boxes of 5.56mm (.223) military ball and boxes of .45 ACP 230-grain full metal case ammo, as well as spare magazines for the pistols and the rifles. For the rifles, the magazines were slightly curving thirty-rounders.

"There are cleaning kits, holsters, webbed belts, bayonets, all else that you might require." The fez-clad man looked very pleased with himself, Frost decided.

"You did good, pal," Frost told him, "but I don't want to know where these came from—promise you won't tell me."

The man laughed, then said, "If I told you, you would be surprised at the legitimacy of the thing. Suffice it to say, they were not stolen from an armory, to my knowledge. And I have the special gun you requested, Captain Frost."

"Where?" Frost asked.

"Here," the man answered, reaching into a small briefcase in the corner of the rear deck.

The gun was something Frost—who prided himself on a knowledge of guns—had never seen before. "What is that?" He recognized the basic gun, but that was all.

"It is one of a specially made group of Heckler & Koch P-7 pistols. There are several exotic variations. This one really isn't that exotic, Captain Frost."

"That silencer looks like an automobile muffler," Frost commented.

"What are you guys talking about?" the girl interjected.

"Here." Frost took the pistol from the man with the fez and showed it to the girl. He inspected it as he did and thought out loud. "Bayonet-type lock for the silencer here—special slide, right?" and he looked at the man with the fez.

"That is correct. There is a standard slide included with the gun for your convenience."

Frost turned the pistol over in his hands.

"Okay, the slide is altered in the front. You put the silencer over the muzzle, twist it into position—now this gadget." Frost studied a small latch at the rear of the silencer, the latch in turn locking into a notch on the side of the slide toward the muzzle of the barrel and the juncture with the silencer itself. "A slide lock—huh? Good," and Frost raised the pistol, pointing it toward the far, empty wall. "I like that," he noted. "The silencer drops below the sighting plane so it doesn't interfere with normal use of the sights." Frost judged the silencer at approximately ten or eleven inches in length. "Is it effective?"

"Exceedingly so—you and the young lady requested a silenced pistol. We chose to provide the very best available. This is from my employer's personal collection."

"A slab-sided silencer—wild," Frost mused.

"I am glad you are pleased. You are familiar with the pistol's basic operating characteristics, Captain Frost?"

Frost nodded, "Squeeze cocker in the front strap of the grip cocks the firing pin, de-cocks it when the gun is released, trigger action drops a firing pin block that prevents discharge otherwise. Eight rounds standard 9mm Parabellum—I like this," Frost smiled.

"Now if you guys are through with this gun stuff, maybe we can get the hell out of here with the equipment—before somebody comes by," the girl almost pleaded.

Frost touched his left hand to her shoulder,

then looked at the man with the fez. "Subsonic ammo too—"

"You would be surprised how effective this is with standard velocity ammunition, but yes, there is a box of forty rounds of subsonic hollow points, specially loaded for your purposes. Is there any other need I or my employer can provide?"

"You got good friends, kid," Frost told Julie Pulman. "Yeah—," he said, then, turning to the man with the fez, "how do we get this out of here?"

"Simply close the packing crates, cover them with the rugs and drive away. I have other transportation."

Frost replaced the pistol in the fitted case, then offered his hand to the man with the fez. "Do you know why we needed all this stuff?"

"It was sufficient for my employer that Miss Pulman rescued his son almost single-handedly from terrorist kidnappers some time ago. And he asked," the fez-clad man said, turning to face Julie Pulman, "that should you ever again, however often, have need of my employers' services, that you never hesitate to contact him. He is forever in your debt for you restored to him that which was most precious."

"Thank you," she smiled, looking embarrassed, Frost thought . . .

It was a long, hot ride across the desert and Frost and Maurice Gilder drove one of the three vehicles in shifts. When Frost opened his eye, Gilder was humming something as the Land Rover bumped and rocked along the road. Frost noted with some disgust that it still wasn't quite dark. "Hey, Maurice," Frost groaned, trying to stretch in the confines of the front seat. "How long have I been asleep?"

"About two hours. I don't mind, really. You've got a rough night waiting for you. Rough indeed, I'd say."

"Yeah," Frost grunted, unfolding a map from the pocket of his bush jacket, studying it a moment, then said, "We pass that oasis yet?"

"Yes—about ten minutes ago. There was no need to stop and the oasis town looked a little crowded to me," Gilder concluded.

"I trust your judgement," Frost told the man. "Well, passing that oasis I make it another sixty miles or so to El Remaka. Then you and I stay outside the action while Julie sets herself up."

"I don't like this—not at all. She risks worse than death."

"I told her that already," Frost told Gilder.

"But she still risks her life. It doesn't make sense."

"Does what we do make sense?" Frost asked Gilder, smiling.

"Ha! I can't argue with logic like yours," Gilder laughed, glancing to his left as he steered the Rover around a pothole.

Julie Pulman had registered under the name Julie Pilsner at the only hotel in El Remaka as a tourist waiting the arrival of her brother. Frost watched the yellow light visible through her curtainless room, knowing she was there, waiting for the strike of the white slavery gang. Frost had studied Julie's reports on the Sheik's tastes—she had made herself perfect. The sheik was a sucker for blonde women, and women travelling alone were so few and far between in the Middle East that, unless the white slavers thought it was too obvious a set-up, they would try for her. It was a perfect chance for them.

Frost, smoking a cigarette, standing in the shadows of a shop door down the block from the hotel and opposite the building on the far side of the street, reached a finger of his left hand up under the burnoose he wore, scratching at his two day growth of beard. Under the robes of the burnoose Frost carried an M-16 bayonet, the H-K pistol with the silencer attached and, just in case, one of the Smith & Wesson Combat Masterpiece four-inch .38 Specials. He hesitated to use one of the available .45 autos until the opportunity arose to test the gun. The H-K he assumed would work—it was from the Greek gunrunner's personal collection. The Smith & Wesson he had dry-snapped, had checked for cylinder lockup, timing, ejector rod wobble— but the gun seemed mechanically perfect. Without testing one of the G.I. issue automatics, though, there was no way to tell just how well they would shoot. They were all loose, unlike the vastly better commercial guns, and Frost had no desire to lob a shot at somebody twenty yards away and miss by a foot.

Maurice Gilder was waiting in the shadows on the opposite side of the street. Should somebody come up to Frost, Frost could answer with one of the Farsi phrases Gilder had taught him. Beyond that Gilder would appear and help out—at least Frost counted on that. Cohn and Miles were waiting behind the hotel, similarly disguised. The other three men in Frost's unit were waiting some slight distance out of town with the vehicles.

There was a low whistling sound from the shadows across the street and Frost drew back into the doorway, dropping the Camel and crushing it under the sole of his combat-booted right foot. The whistle had been from Maurice Gilder and meant someone was coming.

Frost could hear the rumbling noise of a vehicle, and a moment later he saw the slow sweep of headlights on the far side of the street. A vehicle was coming up from Frost's left and heading toward the small hotel. Frost wondered if this was it. They had been waiting in the shadows for almost three hours—Frost checked the face of his Omega and confirmed the timing. In each white slave kidnapping case, the woman apparently had been taken from her hotel room, so Julie waited there. Frost had wanted her to have a gun, but she'd told him no—it would be a dead giveaway. Frost hadn't cared, but the girl had insisted. So now, as the vehicle—a truck—passed in front of Frost and crossed toward Gilder's position, Julie waited alone and unarmed in her room.

There were at least six men in the back of the truck, and two men in the cab. Frost's guts more than anything else told him these were the white slavers and they were pulling up in plain sight in front of the hotel to snatch her. "Damn," he rasped, his right hand under his robe tightening on the butt of the Smith revolver inside the waistband of his fatigue pants.

The truck stopped. The six men got out, dragging after them a large rolled oriental rug. Frost cursed softly under his breath, muttering, "Where's the originality these days?" The man on the passenger side of the cab climbed out of the truck and stood beside the cab. He leaned there and lit a cigarette as the six men from the back walked through the double glass-paneled hotel doors and disappeared into the lobby.

Frost riveted his eye to the yellow-lighted window. He wondered what Julie Pulman was doing—perhaps sitting in bed, reading. She'd be wearing a skimpy nightgown—she'd told Frost that. She wanted to reinforce their desire to take her and to take her undamaged. He felt like a voyeur, watching the window, waiting to see a shadow cross in front of it. He started to light another cigarette, then checked his hand, remembering the man standing beside the truck. Frost froze then as he glanced back up to the window. He could see a single shadow, unmistakably the silhouette of a woman, near the window. He thought he heard a muted scream as the silhouette disappeared from the window, the window going suddenly dark. Frost sucked

69

in his breath hard, wanting to rush from the shadows where he hid, shoot the man beside the truck, rush into the hotel lobby, up the stairs to the second floor room three at a time, crash down the door and drill every one of the six kidnappers. Instead, Frost balled his fists and waited in the darkness, his hands and arms shaking with rage. It was a dumb plan the girl had, Frost thought. And she was dumb to try it—dumb, and at the same time brave.

The light was back on in the room now, but Frost saw nothing in the window. He stared at the black-faced Omega Seamaster 120 on his wrist; it had been five minutes since the light had gone off. Plenty of time for six men to take one woman who wanted to let them take her. He heard a noise, then shifted his gaze to the double hotel doors.

The six men were coming through, carrying a rolled up rug. It seemed a different color than the one they'd carried inside, and the rug bulged oddly. He hoped the girl was all right, and swore to himself that if she weren't he'd get every last man of the white slavery gang.

More carefully than they'd taken the earlier rug from the truck bed, they slung up their new burden and eased it into the truck. Then the men, two at a time, climbed aboard, the man standing beside the truck cab looking the street up and down and snapping his cigarette into the street and climbing aboard the truck.

"Midnight movers," Frost whispered to himself. And the truck was on its way.

70

Frost reached under his robe and snatched the small portable radio set. He turned the volume dial up, then punched down the talk button with his thumb, "One eye to rear element—northbound off objective, one vehicle, no plate visible, two ton approximate, stake truck, no canopy, six—repeat, six personnel in rear, one with driver, subject in rug in truck bed. One eye over."

Frost released the button, holding the set near his ear to hear, "Rear element to one eye—got it—moving out, over."

"One eye—out," Frost snapped, killing the volume button to off. He went out into the street, wanting to run but not daring to. The hotel operator had to be working with the white slavers and if he saw anyone running down the street there might be some way the hotel man had of alerting them—then getting Julie killed. Instead of running Frost walked, slowly, past the hotel glancing casually toward the door, muttering to the unseen hotel proprietor, "Bite it," then moving on.

Frost reached the end of the street, turning slowly, trying to look casual in case anyone was watching. He could see Maurice Gilder, burnoose and robe-clad like himself, shuffling past the hotel doors, using a cane to aid him as he walked. Frost gave credit to Gilder—the man had imagination. Frost turned the corner, not needing to signal to Gilder, walking more quickly now toward the street behind the hotel. He stopped at the corner there. "The hell with it!" he rasped under his breath, then whistled loudly for his two men behind the hotel. The tiny radio he carried had only one channel and—there had been no time to find matching sets—each man could contact the man on the vehicles waiting to receive, but the men could not contact one another. He whistled again, and the two men—Cohn and Miles—ran up the street toward him. Glancing behind him again, Frost could see Gilder, turning the corner and snatching up the cane and breaking into a run.

Frost started running too, away from the hotel, toward the outskirts of the small town—a distance less than two city blocks away—and in the dunes beyond. There two of the vehicles would be waiting. Smith, the driver of the third vehicle, was already tailing the truck carrying Julie Pulman.

As Frost, the others running behind him, reached the edge of the town, he stripped away the burnoose. He ran toward the nearest dunes behind which the vehicles would be, undid the belt around his waist, opened the robe, and stripped it from his shoulders. Bending low into a dead run now he started up the dune, reached the top and started running down, already seeing the second Land Rover and the Travelall at the dune's base, the sounds of the running engines reassuring to him. Frost reached the Land Rover, tossing the burnoose and robe in the back, snatching up his crusher hat and one of the M-16s. Gilder ran up beside him, breathless, and jumped behind the steering wheel.

"All that bookwork gets you out of shape, Gilder," Frost cracked.

Gilder, breathing heavily still, rasped, "Bull-shit, Frost."

As Gilder got the Land Rover moving, the former driver jumped into the back. "Roll it," Luciano shouted, "I got a radio contact with Smith. He's got the vehicle in sight and it seems to be slowing down—maybe stopping."

"Right!" Gilder shouted, cranking the Rover into second, bouncing up along the opposite dune, up and over the top, then wrestling the wheel as the vehicle skidded down the em-bankment and toward the road.

Frost snatched the H-K pistol from his belt, giving the silencer a good luck twist, setting the slide lock. There was static and indistinguish-able radio chatter. Frost shouted to Luciano behind him, "What's up, Luciano?"

"Truck stopped, Captain—he's got 'em in sight and Smith's waiting for us before he moves up."

"Step on it, Maurice," Frost barked to Gilder, the black man beside him grunting some kind of profanity, then punching the stick into third, the engine whining and coughing as the Rover jumped a hummock of dirt and sand and hit the road.

Frost glanced at his watch to mark the time, rotating the movable beezle into position by the current position of the minute hand, then staring down the road. Gilder was running with the parking lights only, and the Travelall behind them was running nearly blind as well. They couldn't risk the lights, and the desert sky, crystal clear and star-filled, seemed—at least to Frost who wasn't doing the driving—to provide adequate illumination.

Frost eared the bolt on the M-16, chambering the top round out of the thirty-round box magazine, then setting the selector to safe. He preferred the heavily customized hybrid M-16 variant he'd used in Monte Azul, but the standard rifle was adequate for his purposes, he decided.

"Gimme one of the shoulder rigs with a .45 and some extra mags," Frost rasped over his shoulder to Luciano, the radio man. Luciano handed over a G.I. leather chest-type shoulder holster, a gun that smelled of oil and four spare magazines. Frost, the vehicle bouncing under him, thumbed out each cartridge in the already loaded magazines, checking the feed lips by feel, checking the spring pressure under the followers, then loaded the magazines each in turn. He slapped the spines of the magazines against the palm of his left hand to seat the rounds they held. He checked the pistol, and because of the dim light, was unable to look down the bore of the Government Auto. Not willing to risk a light from his Zippo, Frost did the best thing he could. He locked the slide back, then blew down the barrel, feeling at the rear of the barrel along the feed ramp with his fingers.

Shrugging, he put one of the magazines up the butt of the GI issue gun, then rammed it locked home. He worked the slide and chambered the first round, then left the pistol cocked and locked, slipping it into the shoulder holster on his chest, then securing the safety strap.

Gilder, his voice loud over the wind rushing past the vehicle, shouted, "You expecting a party Frost, or what—I watched you with that pistol, man."

"Well," Frost answered, staring into the darkness ahead of them, watching the stars occasionally as he looked up, "I been thinkin'. After those white slavers eventually do whatever their deal is with Julie and she's safe and gone—at least safe from gunfire—well, if those guys were to turn up dead, it might just look like a gang rivalry. I don't think it would imperil Julie at all, do you?"

Frost turned, looking at Gilder.

"No, I guess it wouldn't. But what'd you say the numbers were again—forty or so of them?"

"Yeah—more or less," Frost smiled.

"Well, hell! That's less than six to one—ain't it?" Luciano chimed in. Frost looked over his shoulder and laughed, nodding but saying nothing.

"I like your math. Man, you guys are nuts," Gilder laughed. Frost, Gilder and Luciano, still cradling the tiny radio set, were all laughing and Frost, as he automatically checked the road ahead of them thought—at least for a moment— "We're all crazy!"

Frost checked his watch again. "Aren't we almost there, Luciano?"

The radio man responded, "I can't risk calling Smith. What if he's too close for his own good?"

"Yeah," Frost said, then ordered Gilder, "Maurice, stop this thing." Gilder hit the brakes. Frost looked at Gilder, cracking, "Smart ass—you almost put me through the windshield!" Frost piled out of the Land Rover and walked across the sand to a few yards ahead of the vehicle. The Travelall was behind the Rover, both engines throbbing and sounding loud in the clear, calm desert night.

Frost had a gut feeling as he looked out across the vaguely white, shadow-edged dunes. He turned to Maurice Gilder. "Gilder, we're moving out. Luciano, you stay with the vehicles and work the radio for Smith in case he comes in to you." Then, turning his neck further, Frost said, "Bohls, Cohn, Miles—you come with Maurice and me. When we find that spot where they stopped, if a trade takes place and we're sure Julie is going to Ali Hassan Foudani, then we ice those schmucks that took her. No sense letting 'em live to put the bag on some other American girl."

Frost slung the M-16 under his right arm, then waved to his men, "Just like Custer said—follow me, guys." Frost, breaking into a dog trot, started across the sand along the edge of the road, his eye scanning the sand on both sides of the desert track for some sign of automobile tires leaving the highway. He ran on, for what he judged was ten minutes. He almost wished

76

when he stopped that he'd brought a jacket; the desert air that had baked him earlier in the day was now stunningly cold, especially as sweat from the exertion of the run began to dry on his body. He dropped to one knee, inspecting what he thought might be a tire tread. He risked the light of the Zippo's flame. It was a tire tread, the impression heavy as from what he hoped was the truck.

There was no second set of treads crossing it—Smith would have been smart enough to go down a ways, then turn off and parallel his quarry. If there were to be a rendezvous, a second set of tire tracks would be a dead giveaway the truck had been followed.

Frost stood to his full height, turned to Miles and Cohn, and said, "You guys go up the road a ways, intercept Smith's tire tracks and follow them up. We should all wind up the same place. Say nothing within an hour from now"—Frost read his watch aloud—"then break radio silence back to the Rover. We will too, then we can link up. Questions?"

"One, Captain," Caldwell Miles said, his blonde hair falling across his forehead, in his hands an M-16.

"What, Miles?" Frost heard himself almost snap. The timbre of his own voice made him realize just how nervous he was for the Pulman girl's safety.

"If we can't link up, the girl goes, and it's clear to start the—you know—"

"I'll fire the first shot. Go on my lead."

"There are forty of them—maybe that many, Hank," Gilder cautioned.

"I don't care," Frost answered. "If they're standing together it just makes it that much harder to miss when we start shooting. Come on—cut the chit-chat." Frost, with Gilder and Bohls flanking him, started running across the open sand, following the now unmistakable imprint of the white slavers' truck tires.

Glancing at his watch, Frost figured they'd been running for nearly ten minutes. He waved his men to slow down as they approached a long ridge of sand perhaps a hundred yards distant. Using hand and arm signals he fanned Bohls off to the far right flank, keeping Gilder with him as they approached the dunes.

Moving slowly up the sand to the top of the ridge, Frost fell flat on his chest, swinging the M-16 into position, his right eye hard set—he could feel the muscles around it tensing. There were perhaps forty-five men and two women in the dish-like valley beyond the ridge of sand. There were also seven trucks like the rug vendors' truck and the most elaborate Land Rover Frost had ever seen—it looked more like a four-wheel drive limousine.

The passenger door of the Land Rover opened and a burnoose-clad man stepped out, with a neatly trimmed spade beard visible under a strong chin and hawklike nose. He wore military-looking bush clothes and there was a full flap military holster on his right hip. Soon, a driver was beside him and the burnoose-clad man began walking toward the crowd of men and the two women.

Frost pulled the Bushnell armored 8x30s from their case. Swinging them under his right arm, he focused them for his right eye. He thought of Bess and the time she'd made him realize how stupid it was for a one-eyed man to carry binoculars rather than a telescope. Frost wondered if it was part of something inside him—maybe the binoculars were a way of clinging to the days when he hadn't been a one-eyed man. He focused on the man with the white burnoose and the spade beard—the face matched perfectly the face of Ali Hassan Foudani, Sheik of Akaran. Frost swept the binoculars across the valley, toward the women. He dropped the glasses, heard Gilder beside him murmur, "What is it?"

"Nothing—shit." Frost picked up the glasses, blew sand from the objective lenses and studied the two women again. One of them was clearly Julie Pulman, despite the potato sack-like hood covering her head. She was clad only in a torn nightgown, and was visibly shivering. Her hands—Frost focused on them—were handcuffed behind her.

The second woman was the one who had startled him. She wore bush shorts, high khaki-colored socks and sturdy-looking shoes, a short-sleeved white shirt and a bush jacket over her shoulders like a cape. At her hip was a belt, and on it a holster—a pistol clearly in it. In her right hand was a cigarette, and in her left hand was a submachine gun of some sort. Frost guessed it was an UZI.

"I'll be damned," he whispered, half to himself and half to Gilder.

"Let me see, Frost." Frost handed the binoculars to Gilder.

"You see—the second woman down there."

"That guy—it's the Sheik—he just walked over to her and shook her hand. They're talking, almost like she's helping him inspect the Pulman woman."

"Here—gimme." Frost took the binoculars back, studying the scene unfolding below him. To anyone it would have been obvious: the woman wearing the pistol belt and holding the submachine gun so casually and naturally was the leader of the white slavery gang. Frost studied her in more detail. She was dark-haired, perhaps American, or at least European. Over the dark hair she had tied a multi-colored scarf, Gypsy fashion.

He watched as the woman stubbed out her cigarette under her foot in the sand, then with a certain amount of dramatic flourish, pulled the bag off Julie Pulman's head.

He watched as the other woman roughly took Julie's jaw in her right hand, forcing the lips open. The Sheik inspected the teeth, as if he were buying a horse. The Sheik nodded, in evident approval, then gestured toward Julie's body. The other woman nodded and slung the sub gun across her back, then with both hands reached up to the neckline of Julie's nightgown and ripped. Frost could hear, faintly, the tearing sound across the quiet desert.

And Julie stood there, naked. Frost raised the binoculars to Julie's face—either she was a good actress or she really was, by now, terrified.

The sheik walked slowly around her, feeling occasionally at her thighs, at her left breast. He dropped to a crouch, and nearly knocking Julie down, lifted her left foot, apparently inspecting it.

Ali Hassan Foudani stood then, nodded slowly, then without as much as a second glance to the handcuffed, naked woman he'd just minutely looked over, he began to walk toward his Land Rover with the dark-haired woman. Frost watched them. They were talking animatedly, and once the dark-haired woman gestured back toward Julie.

The Sheik shook his head no to something, then started to board his Rover. The woman touched his coat sleeve. Frost watched the Sheik's eyes; he looked like he'd kill the woman for touching him. She drew her hand away a moment, looked back over her shoulder toward Julie, then nodded.

The Sheik's face visibly lit with enthusiasm and he turned and said something to his driver. The driver started to fish in his pockets and produced a roll of bills. Frost decided it was a cash and carry operation.

The woman—the leader—shouted something barely audible to Frost, and two of the men of the white slavery gang ran over to Julie. One of them stuffed a rag in her mouth, then the other wrapped a blanket around her, snatched her up into his arms and ran across the sand.

The Sheik's driver stood by the rear of the Rover and had the deck open. He helped the white slaver to sling Julie into the back of the vehicle. The driver produced a length of rope, tied Julie's bare ankles, then shoved the ankles inside. The driver ran around the side of the Rover, hopped aboard and the Rover started to move in the opposite direction.

As soon as the Rover vanished over the far ridge of sand, Frost—almost amused—watched the woman who had just sold Julie raise the middle finger of her right hand in a salute and even from the distance of the ridge where he hid, Frost could hear laughter among the forty or so white slavers.

Frost hoped they'd wait a while and count the money, recount old times—something to get the Sheik far enough away before the shooting started.

Frost studied his watch, hearing Gilder whisper, "What if Miles and Cohn aren't in position?"

"Well—I guess we might get killed then," Frost whispered back, then added, "But look, Maurice—it's been swell knowing you all these years."

"Bullshit—"

"Well, that too," Frost answered thoughtfully.

Gilder looked at Frost, shaking his head disgustedly, then Gilder said, "Crazy white man!"

Frost studied the watch, glancing back through the binoculars, then looking down the ridge line to his right, seeing Bohls in position a hundred and fifty yards away.

Frost looked through the binoculars again, scanning the camp. There were no heavy weapons visible, but he didn't discount their presence because of that. One of the seven trucks could have concealed a machine gun under a tarp.

The white slaver gang was starting to break up, to head for the trucks. Frost checked his watch and saw ten minutes had passed. The knot of men around the woman leader starting to break up as well, and the woman—in masculine broad strides—moved across the valley.

"Okay, Gilder," Frost said and snugged the M-16 to his shoulder and opened fire with a short, three-round burst, killing a man just climbing into a truck cab. Nothing happened for what seemed to Frost like an eternity, but he realized it was likely less than a second. Faces stared toward the ridge line where Frost and Gilder were, where Frost had fired from. There was a shout, then Frost shouted "All hell's breakin' loose, Maurice!" Guns were going off from the valley floor, but bodies were falling there, too. Frost realized Miles and Cohn and probably Smith had made it into position and were following his lead. There was a loud, mechanical spitting sound from beside Frost and he felt hot brass brush against his bare fore-

83

arm and his cheek. Gilder was firing and Frost, settling the M-16 tight in his shoulder cup, started a string of three-shot bursts, burning out his first magazine, watching as the bodies fell, slamming a fresh magazine home in the assault rifle and continuing to fire.

"Let's go," Frost shouted, starting up to his feet, hearing Gilder muttering something with the word "crazy" in it. But Frost was already over the ridge line and starting down toward the valley, firing the M-16 from his hip like a submachine gun. Shifting another magazine in place, he switched the M-16 into his right hand, took the Smith & Wesson Combat Masterpiece in his left hand, and fired both guns as he ran straight into the valley. He heard a shout from the far side on the opposite ridge, and saw Miles, Cohn and Smith running into the valley too, their M-16s blazing fire in the night.

One of the white slavers was charging toward Frost, a long, heavy bladed knife in his hands. Frost wheeled, firing the M-16 and the Smith revolver simultaneously, catching the white slaver in the chest and throat, the man bouncing up into the air, spinning and spread-eagling into the sand. Frost stepped on the body as he continued running into the valley, seeing Bohls on his far right, Maurice Gilder with his M-16 spitting neat, three-round bursts, walking slowly down the dunes, firing into a solid flank of the white slaver gang.

Frost fired the Smith revolver again, nailing another of the gang members in the face. Then the six-shot wheelgun was empty and Frost crammed it into his belt, ramming a fresh magazine into the M-16, then shifting the gun to his left hand. He snatched the cocked and locked .45 from the shoulder rig, thumbing down the safety, then fired it. The Government Model was in his right fist, the pistol grip on the M-16 in his left, both guns spitting gilding metal jacketed lead, cutting through a wall of the white slavers.

And as the wall started crumbling, Frost could see, on the far edge of the impromptu battleground, the woman—running, dodging, shooting, heading toward one of the trucks.

Frost shot out the .45 and rammed it back in the leather. He started to run, buttstroking a big, burly man with the M-16, then ramming the flash deflector into the man's nose and pulling the trigger, splitting the head wide, almost breaking his own wrists from the heightened recoil, and Frost was running again.

The woman was mounting the truck, and apparently seeing Frost, fired a long burst from her submachine gun. Frost piled into the sand, rolling, the sand spitting up in a ragged line to his right as he rolled left. He stopped, on his back, the M-16 over him and he fired as the woman started into the truck. Pumping the trigger, in and out, in and out, he got off two three-round bursts. He rolled onto his stomach, and the woman still stood on the running board of the truck cab, her back to him. As she turned to face him, as she had been when he'd fired,

Frost could see her. The front of her chest and her neck were a bloody pulp, her right hand dropped the sub gun, then went up to touch the wounds. Her body keeled over, falling face down and limp like a bag of rags, into the sand.

Frost pushed himself to his feet, the fighting still raging around him. He loaded a fresh magazine into the M-16 and sprayed three men starting out of the valley. They dropped and already, as Frost and his men finished the job, Frost knew there was only one thing remaining to do: stake out the Palace where Julie Pulman was to be held—then sweat it out and wait.

Chapter Eight

"This is the most sophisticated surveillance stuff I've seen since Nam," Gilder observed.

Frost looked at the man, saying, "Well, you'll have to compliment Julie on it. It's her stuff."

"First class, I tell you," Gilder noted. He paused, then said, "It's been three days, Frost— not a damned thing unusual. I've been hanging around close to the palace all I can. It doesn't make any sense. If she were going to get a message out . . . well."

Frost answered, "She expected him to use drugs. Maybe he's got her sedated and she can't. Yeah, I'm antsy too, though." He slid back under the curtain and out of the velvet blackness of the observation tent and into the sun-filled adobe-like room. It took a while for his eye to get accustomed to the greater light.

Part of the reason for the observation tent was to allow the ultra-sophisticated optics maximum light-gathering ability and allow the viewing eye the minimum light distraction. The room, Frost reflected, as he walked toward the small balcony and stared out onto the crowded street of the capitol of Akaran, was a half-mile from the palace. He had selected the place because of its uninterrupted view of the palace, despite the distance. Comings and goings at the main gate could be seen clearly, the side gate partially. It was also possible to spy—at least to a degree—on the gardens outside the royal apartments. Occasionally someone could be seen walking there and once—though proven a false hope—they had seen what appeared to be a woman in a classic, diaphanous harem outfit walking in the garden. Perhaps it had been a member of Ali Hassan Foudani's harem, but it had neither been Julie nor Louise Canaretti.

Frost lit a cigarette and walked back to the low table they used as a desk. He sat on the slightly moldy-smelling couch and studied the notebooks on the table. There were street observations, observations through the surveillance equipment, and even records of snatches of conversation picked up in and near the palace area by the ultra-sensitive parabolic microphone Frost and his men employed. But there was still nothing giving fresh insight into either the location or condition of either of the American women.

Frost hammered his fist down on the desk, then heard Gilder's voice, muffled-sounding from inside the tent, "It won't do you any good to get angry, Hank. I'm going to go back out into the street and try to get near the palace and see what I can—hey—it's those funny guys again! Come take a look!"

Frost killed the cigarette, then crossed the room and slid back under the tent, muttering, "Coming through!" so Gilder would close his eyes a moment when the light penetrated the blackness.

Frost's own eye accustomed to the darkness once again, and he fumbled to the scope and adjusted the focus for himself. They had watched the two men several times over the three days of observation. Both of them were European, one was rather old, the other perhaps in his twenties. There was something odd about the men, but Frost couldn't peg it. The men would leave in the morning, then return later in the day, each time going out in a freshly washed and polished car. They returned in the same car but it was covered with dust from the desert. Once Frost had caught a detailed look at the way the one man was dressed—desert camie fatigues and a pistol in a shoulder holster. And yet, he thought, there was still something peculiar about the men, something indefinable, something—the thought bothered him—frightening.

Frost rasped to Gilder, "Maurice, get Luciano and Bohls up here on this. Contact Smith to get one of the cars cranked up. We're going out into the desert after those guys. I want to see what they're up to."

"None of our business, Frost, you know?"

"Yeah—just do it anyway—okay?"

"Right," Gilder snapped. Frost still watched the two men as their car began moving away from the palace gates, hearing Gilder rustling through the curtain . . .

The ride into the desert had been hot and long—and tedious. Each time they approached a ridge of sand, they would stop, Frost or Gilder or Smith running up to the top of the ridge to make certain the four wheel drive vehicle the men had transferred to just outside the capitol city wasn't parked on the other side of the ridge. Frost had no desire to run up on the two men and their Arab driver. Frost, Gilder and Smith took turns also, one of them perpetually leaning from the back of the Rover and swishing a large towel across the sand behind the vehicle to obliterate as much of the track they left behind as possible—that was the hottest and dirtiest of the jobs.

Frost came off duty on the "towel patrol" as the three men had taken to calling it, then heard Gilder, who was driving, say, "Got another ridge up ahead—tracks going over it."

Frost nodded, more to himself than to Gilder, who wasn't looking. "Smith—hey Sunshine!"

"Yeah, Captain?"

"Go on up there and take a look—your turn next on this thing." Frost threw the towel down in disgust, swatting at his trouser legs and shirt with his crusher hat as he walked forward. He leaned against the side of the Rover, then quickly backed away from it—the metal was burning hot under the sun.

As Smith started up the dune ridge, there was a shot in the distance. Frost dropped to a crouch and snatched at the Combat Masterpiece in his trouser band, the grips wet with sweat from being under his shirt.

Smith was prone on the sand, an M-16 in his right fist. There was another shot, then another, but the shots were clearly not aimed at them, Frost decided. He signalled to Gilder and Frost, who started together up the ridge of sand, dropping low beside Smith. "What the hell is it?"

"I don't know, Captain—it's from over there." Smith gestured beyond the top of the ridge.

Frost, nodding, got up into a low crouch, and dropping to his knees, started up the sand dune. A dozen yards below the top he crawled the rest of the way, finally on his belly on the baking hot sand as he peered over the top of the ridge.

He signalled to Gilder and Smith to follow, then stared back over the ridge. He glanced skyward, confirming the omnipresent sun, then dismissed the idea of using his binoculars as the objective lenses might catch the sun and betray his position.

As Gilder and Smith joined him, Frost tried assessing what he saw at the far edge of the shallow sandy valley near the opposite ridge. There was an elaborate wooden-looking facade, supposedly of buildings, he guessed, but odd-shaped buildings, with bizarre and crudely shaped statuary. They were obviously meant to represent something. There was a speaker's platform of some type or reviewing stand near the buildings. There was a flagged-off area, several department store-type dummies standing near the flagged-off area and several more of the manniquins on the platform. One of them was wearing a business suit—already visibly faded in the sun—standing at the center of the platform.

Yes, Frost decided. Definitely a speaker's platform—the thing behind which the business suited dummy was propped had to be a podium of sorts. It had a plexiglass partition atop the flat surface partially shielding the face of the dummy from the other dummies on the far side beyond the flagged-off area. Scanning further away from the platform, there was a high wooden scaffolding and there were two men coming down from it now, the one with a submachine gun and the other with a rifle. The two men were dressed in military fatigues and berets, but the distance was too great for Frost to determine what, if any, insignia they wore.

He rolled over on his back, avoiding looking up at the sun, and studied the toes of his boots instead. He said to Gilder, "Those guys are rehearsing an assassination. You agree?"

"Yes—but for whom, I wonder," Gilder said.

"Watch it with that 'whom,'" Frost wise-cracked. "Your superior education is showing again."

"Sorry," Gilder apologized.

Frost rolled back onto his stomach and watched the scene in the valley. He could clearly see the younger of the two men they had followed walking up onto the speaker's platform, approach the podium, then take a riding crop or stick and hit the plexiglas shielding. The man turned to the two men in fatigues, standing on the far side of the flagged-off area and did something Frost was sure he was misinterpreting—it looked like a World War II vintage Nazi salute.

Chapter Nine

"What the hell you think those guys were doing? I mean, it certainly seemed as though it were a—"

"I know what it seemed like, Maurice," Frost answered, sipping at a cup of overly thick coffee, looking over the small cup and at the crowded restaurant floor. "You find out anything by the palace?" he asked and looked at Gilder.

Like himself, Gilder was dressed in a long, scraggly burnoose and seen-better-days robe. Frost had elected to meet Gilder away from the rented room with the observation equipment on the off chance Gilder might have been spotted or followed. They had sat in the small, grubby restaurant for nearly twenty minutes, but none of the scores of the Sheik's soldiers or secret police had arrived.

"I found out nothing," Gilder said, the positive tone of his voice somehow disturbing. "We

94

should have had a better contact system. I should have tried getting on the kitchen staff or something. They could always use people."

"And you could always get killed, too. No. I made up my mind, after that dress rehearsal for an assassination this afternoon. This whole set-up stinks. I'm going to do what I should have done all along. I'm going in and getting her out. You or any of the guys don't feel like coming, I won't blame you. You'll be smart."

"You like the Pulman girl, huh?"

"Yeah," Frost murmured, dying for a cigarette, but not wanting to attract attention to himself by smoking. Not many others in the restaurant smoked. "It's not anything really because I've got the hots for her or anything, either— although she's a hell of a girl. But—well—"

"Spit it out, Hank," Gilder said.

"Well—I was thinking. You, me—any of us. We're expected to do the rough and tough number. We're men. That goes with the physical equipment. You wonder though, with a dame like this Julie Pulman. Is she so brave— she is brave, stupid too to be that brave, but brave—is she that way because guys like us make her have to be that way?"

"What do you mean?"

"Well, you think about it. If somebody told you you were going to meet a private detective who was one of the top paid experts in the field in the whole world, had shot it out with terrorists, kidnappers—the whole nine yards—well—"

"I'd expect a man, you mean?"

"Look at yourself," Frost began. "Why'd you work so hard in school? You got a Ph.D., you've written some books. But why did you push so hard?"

"I guess because I was black."

"Well, I rest my case. Maybe she had to be the first one over the top just to make it over the top at all. If she wanted to do okay in her profession, she had to be ten times better than good. She had to be the best or nobody'd take her seriously. Hell, why wasn't she making babies or being somebody's secretary? You know?"

"You a women's libber now?"

"No, it isn't that," Frost said, looking at Gilder. "I just wonder if—"

"You try so hard because of the eye, I try hard because I'm black, she tries so hard because she's a woman in a man's job?"

"Something like that, yeah," Frost nodded. "Let's get out of here. I'm going in tonight and bust her out. The hell with this."

As Frost started to get up, he felt Gilder's hand on his arm. "Count me in—I'm stupid too."

"Thanks," Frost murmured.

Chapter Ten

The customs man, looking at Frost's luggage, had given him an odd stare—there had been two black silk scarves in the luggage. Frost had told the man, not knowing if he understood English well enough to know what Frost was talking about, "I'm planning to break my arm and supply my own sling." The man had closed the suitcase and given Frost another odd stare.

Now, one of the black scarves was tied across Frost's hair, like a gypsy, the other tied across his face like a mask. His forehead was itching from his dark camouflage make-up that killed the shine there. His hands were in dark brown cloth gloves, the fingers cut out. He wore tight but comfortable black jeans, cinched into the tops of his combat boots. A black long-sleeved knit shirt finished the night outfit.

There was no sense carrying a rifle, Frost had decided. Instead, he had his own bayonet and another bayonet borrowed from Gilder. One was strapped to each side of his trouser belt, its web-belt hangars taped to avoid sound. The H-K P7 with the silencer attachment and three extra magazines was his primary weapon until he could steal a submachine gun inside the palace grounds. The Smith Combat Masterpiece was rammed inside his trouser band under the shirt. He carried spare ammo between pieces of black masking tape in rows of six. A "six-pack" was in each of the side and hip pockets of his pants.

There was a two hundred yard expanse of bare ground between the palace wall and the shadowed doorway where Frost stood. His burnoose and robe were in a heap on the floor. They had covered the ninja gear until he'd crossed through the town and to the walls.

Gilder and the others would be coming, but not for a time. It was up to Frost to get inside and find the women; he wanted both Julie Pulman and the Canaretti girl before too much shooting started. He checked his wristwatch—twenty minutes remained before Gilder would take Bohls, Miles, Luciano, Smith and Cohn and begin a noisy assault on the side gate.

Frost glanced up and down the street, side to side, then checked the H-K, the slide lock secured for almost totally silent shooting with the subsonic ammo carried in the eight round magazines.

He started to move, then caught himself a moment. A smile crossed his lips under the bandanna mask. Life had stepped in and prevented him from even thinking much about Bess and himself, what had worried him so on the airplane. He wondered about the brown-haired woman too—the one who'd saved his life, Fran Hood. If this job came off, he thought, there would be three hundred and fifty thousand dollars, all safe in Switzerland. It was enough for a prudent man, who invested his funds wisely, to live on for the rest of his life—if he had a life to live.

Frost felt amused at the thought—Hank Frost, a prudent man! It was easier for him, he realized then, to take a gun in his fist, or a knife in his hand and go fight somebody who had committed some obvious wrong. It was easier for him to circumvent the gritty stuff of life— the work, the detail, the boredom, the lack of success. In his business, he thought, if you didn't succeed you didn't have to worry about living with failure—or living, period.

Simplistic, he thought. Someone had called him that once. And he was. Good, bad, success or death. Simple choices, and he liked them.

He glanced at the black-faced Omega on his left wrist, the band taped over with black masking tape to kill the reflection of the stainless steel band. "Here I go again," he muttered to himself. Glancing up and down the street, he broke into a low, dead run from the shadows and across the open area toward the palace wall.

If there were a sentry looking from behind the latticework of the wall, he'd be shot before he ever stopped running. He kept running, out of breath, sucking air through the suddenly suffocating mask over his face and mouth as he flattened himself against the palace grounds wall. So far, he thought, so good.

Miles, Caldwell Miles, famous stunt man, had taught him the next part. Frost reached into a large bag near his left side pocket, pulling out what looked like a cross between ice skates and climber's spikes. He squatted in the dust by the wall, and affixed the devices to the fronts of his combat boots. A small spike extended three-quarters of an inch outward, then Frost ran the rest of each unit under the soles of his footgear, securing them behind the heel of each boot. He tied them securely. Tiny spikes now ringed each foot cleat on the soles of each boot. From the same bag, he pulled similar rigs for each hand. Then he discarded the bag in the shadows. He'd tried carrying a pistol with the spiked climbing apparatus in place, but it wasn't possible. He hoped he wouldn't need a gun until he got over the wall.

He'd tried climbing the wall of the rented room, and the devices had worked, but only three feet up to the twelve-foot ceiling. Miles had told him that if he balanced carefully the devices could allow him to crawl across the ceiling—Frost had decided not to try that. He wondered if all these years his trepidations about flying were because of a latent fear of heights? He shrugged, got up to his feet and moved awkwardly along the wall, looking for the best spot according to what Miles had told him. Walking with the spikes on his boots was difficult, like walking on sponges.

Once, he'd had his feet too closely together and gotten the spikes hooked together, almost cutting off a finger trying to pry them apart. He stopped beside the wall, raising his right foot and punching the spikes into the wall surface and cracks. He raised his left hand, then extended his right hand upward and got a hold. "What the hell," he muttered to himself, pushing up with his left foot, pulling with his right hand, bracing with the opposite hand and foot. He stopped and closed his eye, then looked down. "Son of a gun," he swore, smiling—it had worked, and he was already two feet above the street level.

He did the routine again, methodically because he really didn't understand it, and moved upward again—he tried to remember the name of the comic book character who climbed walls. In a way, he thought, it was almost fun. He looked down—"Mistake," he muttered to himself—and found he was halfway up the thirty-foot wall. There was still no sign of a guard.

Frost kept moving.

Frost's right hand finally reached the top of the wall and he stopped. He would have to navigate the wrought iron grillwork at the top and swing over before ditching the climbing gear. He started up, stopping with his eye at the level of the grillwork. He saw nothing beyond it, then started to climb again. The spikes were no longer of any use, and, in fact, hindered him as they caught in the iron grillwork and from time to time clanged against it. The grillwork was eight feet high and, stopping at the top before peering over, Frost looked down—thirty-eight feet to the ground. "Yuck!" he snarled. He peered over the top of the grillwork, saw nothing and started clamboring over. The spikes on his left foot stuck for a moment. He edged back, awkwardly, got his foot clear, and swung both legs over the top. He started down, not wanting to drop because of the noise the spikes would make. His feet firmly planted on the guardwalk along the wall, he leaned against the grillwork, breathing a heavy sigh of relief.

"Who—"

At least he thought I was an American and used English, Frost thought in a flash as he wheeled around, slapping out with his spiked left hand at the guard less than three feet from him on the edge of the shadow. Frost caught the man full in the face with the spike, then dived on him to finish him and silence him. Frost's right knee smashed up into the side of the guard's head and there was a low moan. All movement stopped. With the tips of his fingers, Frost felt for a pulse—there was none.

His eye well-accustomed to the shadowy darkness, Frost searched the man after stripping away the climbing gear from his hands and feet—he hid it behind a potted date palm on the walkway of the wall. The man wore a short, broad-bladed sword—something a pirate might be expected to carry. He also had a Beretta Brigadier—the old Model 1951 9mm single action semi-automatic—and carried no submachine gun; that disappointed Frost—he'd wanted to secure one.

Frost stuffed the Beretta into his trouser band beside the Smith revolver, searched the dead man and found no spare magazines for the pistol. He tried to remember the magazine capacity—eight or nine, he thought, making a mental note to check later if he got the opportunity.

He left the sword with the climbing gear behind the date palm, then pushed the body as close to the grillwork as possible, hoping the guard wouldn't be missed.

Frost started along the walkway, hugging the spidery shadows of the grillwork. His eye glanced into the courtyard below and the garden beyond it, having pegged it as the harem area. Now, seeing armed guards outside the garden gates, he determined his earlier supposition was correct.

Frost rolled back the sleeve of his black knit shirt, exposing the luminous face of the Omega wristwatch—ten minutes remained until Gilder and the others would start their attack. He rolled the sleeve back over the watch, searching the walkway for a way down into the courtyard thirty feet below. He found one twenty yards to his left and, as quickly as possible, made for it, the H-K pistol that the Beretta had replaced in his belt in his right fist.

Frost stopped by the long, sloping stairs, listening, watching the shadowy garden below. There was light streaming from a broad veranda area to his right, a few hundred yards distant from the harem enclosure. Frost, taking the steps slowly in the darkness, hugging the wall to keep into the shadow, started down, then across the garden. He ran, zig-zagging between the shrubs and plants and decorative stone sculptures, toward the veranda.

Frost ducked into the shadow of a tall standing palm. Three guards, similarly armed to the man Frost had killed, walked by him, uncomfortably close. As soon as the men were past, Frost dodged from the shadows, toward the veranda. He flipped a low railing and dropped flat behind a hedgerow, hardly daring to breathe lest he be heard. Glancing from side to side, Frost started up onto his hands then on his hands and knees. In a low crouch, he ran behind the hedgerow, into a stand of palms and low, broadleafed plants he didn't recognize—he hoped they weren't the local variety of poison ivy.

Moving slowly, carefully through the foilage, Frost stopped again, ducking down behind one of the unidentified plants, listening. He could hear voices on the veranda and, parting two of the broad green leaves, he could see the Sheik, Ali Hassan Foudani, sitting at the head of a long table, and the two men from the assassination rehearsal. Nazis? He wondered, the salute still bothering him. He watched as the Sheik lifted a glass in a toast. Frost vaguely remembered Moslems weren't supposed to drink. Then Frost decided that had Foudani been a good Moslem, he wouldn't have been kidnapping women for a harem and Frost wouldn't have had to be there.

Shrugging, Frost hoped they'd enjoy a long dinner. He glanced at his watch. At least seven minutes longer.

The harem enclosure was to his immediate left, its nearest gate two hundred yards along the garden. Working his way through the foliage, then to the hedgerow, Frost kept to a low crouch, running as quickly as he could, dropping flat and holding his breath as three more guards walked past on the other side of the hedgerow.

He glanced at his watch. The guards stopped, conversing in a mixture of English words with Farsi the basic tongue—or at least Frost guessed it was Farsi. He smiled, thinking, Farsi is Greek to me. He shook his head. As the guards walked on, Frost started to his feet again, jumping the hedgerow and getting into another tall stand of palms, with more of the mysterious broad-leafed plants. Ducking down, moving in a slow, low crouch, he edged toward the harem enclosure—a high fence of wrought iron grillwork, perhaps twenty feet high. Beyond the fence were glass-panelled doors. These were hung with nearly transparent drapes in a variety of pastels.

Hugging the bottom of the grillwork, Frost worked his way forward toward the nearest gate.

Looking ahead, he spotted two burly guards, both of them apparently armed only with pistols and the peculiar swords.

Frost stopped as close to the guards as he could, debating whether he could take them both silently. He glanced at the Omega on his wrist. Four minutes or so remained. There was no time, he thought, for finesse. He looked at the H-K, the silenced pistol molded into his right fist.

Hoping the subsonic ammo would properly cycle the pistol, he released the slide lock. Total silence would have to be sacrificed for rapid shot placement. He judged each of the guards as pushing two hundred and fifty pounds, more like wrestlers in size than soldiers. One subsonic 9mm on somebody that size was more than dicey. He smiled at himself, though. There wasn't any other choice.

Chapter Eleven

Frost stepped out of the shadows, less than ten feet from the two guards, rasping, "Hey—sissy!"

The nearer of the two guards wheeled, the right hand reaching for the sword rather than the Beretta on his right hip. Frost shoved the silenced H-K out straight in front of him, stamping down his right foot as he did, firing the pistol as it settled on line, the discharge sounding like a loud belch. The hollow-point slug drilled a third eye in the middle of the nearest guard's forehead.

Frost wheeled, the second guard starting to open his mouth to sound an alarm, reaching for the Beretta on his hip. Frost fired once, the round slamming with visible impact into the guard's open mouth, teeth and blood vomiting from the crimson red mouth. The man, already starting into a forward motion before Frost had pulled the trigger, lurched backward from the

107

hips up, the legs flying out from under him, the body crashing downward. Frost wheeled, moving the silencer's muzzle across the garden like a wand, searching for anyone who had come running upon hearing the subdued shots. There was no one.

There was no time to drag the bodies away, the guards being just as conspicuous absent as dead, Frost decided. He snatched both of the Beretta pistols, shoving one behind his right kidney, one behind the left under his shirt, searching the bodies quickly for keys to the wrought iron gates. There were none. He realized the guards were there, but not trusted to stay out themselves. "Damnit," Frost said under his breath, looking up to the top of the gate. The gates themselves were only fifteen feet or so high.

"Wonderful," he said half-aloud, then started toward the gate. The H-K crowded into his belt with the rest of the hardware already there, he started climbing, the handholds easy, the foot placement difficult. Once, halfway up, his right foot stuck in the grillwork, wedged solidly. It took, he judged, almost a minute of twisting and pulling to get it free. He moved more carefully after that, reaching the top of the gate, tempted to jump and save time, then reminding himself a broken ankle wouldn't save time at all.

He started climbing down, jumping the last seven feet, going down into a crouch and snatching the H-K from his belt; the length of the pistol with the silencer had nearly ruptured him when he'd hit the ground.

Moving the gun along the interior courtyard, seeing nothing, Frost took off in a dead run for the glass doors, assuming the harem to be beyond.

He reached the doors, stopped and glanced at his watch. Two minutes remained until Gilder and the others started their combination assault and diversion. He tried the glass door. As he'd expected, it wouldn't budge. Shaking his head, he stepped back. He'd have to smash the glass, and likely there was an alarm system on it, and even if there weren't, the sound of the glass shattering would bring people. And it wouldn't be long until the two guards he'd killed were discovered, or maybe the earlier guard on top of the wall.

"Why not," he said aloud, sighing hard, taking the Smith & Wesson from his belt then thinking better of it. He took one of the Berettas, and checked the chamber. It was empty.

He assumed they were all carried that way. "Dumb!" he muttered. He jacked back the slide on the stolen pistol, aimed it toward the bottom of the glass door and hoped no one was standing behind it. He pulled the trigger, the glass shattered and the weight of the glass above the hole caused the whole piece of plate glass to shard and sliver and collapse. There was a woman's scream from inside. He assumed, at least, he'd found the right place—the harem.

Chapter Twelve

Frost stepped through the doorway, light streaming toward him. The harem—women—were in costumes that looked like they belonged in a burlesque theater. They ran in all directions, screaming.

"Julie," Frost shouted at the top of his lungs, half-jogging across the blue-tiled floor, past a fountain, and ripping aside more of the diaphonous curtains. He could hear gunfire from the outside of the harem enclosure. He glanced at his watch. Gilder was right on time.

"Julie! Miss Canaretti!" Frost stopped, wheeling, guards streaming toward him from a far door in the palace side of the harem. He fired the Beretta and the H-K in perfect unison, nailing the lead man twice, knocking him back into the man behind him.

Frost started into a run, emptying the first Beretta at two more of the guards, one of them brandishing a sword, throwing the gun at a third man when it ran dry.

He snatched another of the Berettas from his belt, jacked back the slide, and continued firing.

The harem itself was broken into tiny curtained rooms with the main hall of the enclosure cut off. Frost edged toward the nearest of the rooms, hacking down the curtain with the silenced H-K pistol. Two women were hiding there, and screamed as he passed, shouting something—he assumed it was Farsi for something he didn't want to know. He shoved into the next enclosure, getting his pistol caught up in the curtain, ripping it free, wheeling just in time and shooting another guard. He could hear more assault rifle fire from outside the enclosure by the side entrance to the palace grounds. He heard the sounds of explosions, too. Somehow Julie had acquired grenades independently of the Greek gunrunner and his fez-hatted salesman, and Gilder and the others had them. There was another explosion. Frost didn't give it too many more minutes before the Army and the Secret Police would be on their tails as well.

He shoved through into another of the curtained rooms. There were eight more of the wrestler-sized guards running for him, one of them—the one in the lead—twirling one of the massive, short swords, high over his head, like a majorette would twirl a baton in a homecoming parade.

"Wonderful," he commented, shooting the lead man in the face twice, then emptying the

111

second Beretta and snatching at the third one. Pistol shots rang into the wall behind him, chipping chunks of tile down on him. Frost dove behind a row of brightly colored cushions, firing back, nailing two more men. He fired the H-K pistol as well until it was finally empty.

More of the guards were coming as Frost rammed the empty H-K into his belt grabbing for the last Beretta.

He got to his feet and ran through another of the curtained rooms. He dived again as a hail of pistol fire rang against the tiled walls. He ripped away the bandanna covering his face and the one covering his hair—the camouflage make-up made his forehead itch. On both knees, behind some cushions, Frost fired as the guards rushed him, emptying the last Beretta and now emptying the Smith & Wesson revolver. He threw away the Beretta, fumbling in his pockets for one of the six packs of .38 Special rounds. He started to reload as he ran, half-tripping over the body of one of the guards.

On his knees, a sword wielding man more massive than any of the other pursuers, screamed something that sounded wholly unpleasant even though Frost couldn't understand it. Frost had the .38 Special rounds in his hand, with no time to reload the H-K. He had the tape stripped away from the .38 cartridges, but the man was closing on him. He heard the word, "American!" shouted like something that meant something dirty.

Frost threw the loose .38 Special rounds into

the man's face and the man shifted away, slowing his charge. Frost looked down to the dead guard beside him. The pistol was nowhere in sight, so Frost grabbed the sword. Getting to his feet, he backed away, looked at the sword and asked himself aloud, "What am I doing!?"

The guard was charging again, a smile on the man's lips, the word "American" shouted again like a curse, Frost thought. He told himself, "This is really a funny rifle with a funny bayonet. Oh, my God!" Frost swung the sword, his blade locking against the blade of the monster-sized harem guard.

"Anyone ever tell you you've got bad breath, Charlie?" Frost rasped, his face inches from that of the guard.

Frost fell back, rolling as the man cleaved downward with the sword. Frost swung the blade horizontally toward the man's knees, the man jumping back. Frost started to run, the big man behind him.

There were guns going off outside, more explosions as well. There were women in what looked like pervert underwear to Frost, running everywhere, screaming.

Frost kept running, reaching another section of the harem. He stopped, trying to steady his hand enough to fumble for a fresh magazine for the H-K. But the guard—despite his size—was fast and before Frost could get the pistol and the magazine together, Frost had to dodge, the magazine in his teeth now, the pistol rammed back into his belt. He swung the sword, missing

113

the Arab harem guard completely, the big man laughing.

Frost pulled the H-K magazine from his teeth and rasped, "You bastard—I wish you understood English," then swung the heavy sword again.

As the Arab slashed the sword right to left and then down, Frost caught the blade with his own, the impact knocking him to his knees. As the Arab sliced downward with the sword, Frost half-rolled. He caught the sword again, then pushed himself up to his feet, the swords locked, the big man throwing his weight against Frost. Frost rolled away to his knees, hacking wildly with the sword as the big man dodged, then came for him. Frost got to his feet again, swinging the sword to keep the harem guard at bay.

"An American!"

Frost wheeled and saw a blonde-haired woman dressed like the other women in the harem. It wasn't Julie—he decided it had to be Louise Canaretti.

Frost started to turn, saw the sword blade crashing downward on him and ducked, hitting the tiled floor and sliding as the big Arab hacked with his sword.

Getting to his feet, backing away, Frost glanced toward the woman again.

"Louise—Louise Canaretti?"

"Yeah—damned right," the girl shouted back. And then Frost froze. There was another woman, beside whom she knelt, blonde like she was. The eyes were closed, the skin pale. It was

114

Julie Pulman and she was unconscious.

Frost sidestepped as the big Arab swung his sword again. Frost rolled to the floor, wheeling on his knees as the Arab swung for him again, hacking through one of the sheer curtains, the curtain falling. Frost got to his feet, hacking away, feeling something behind his legs, the sword blade crashing down as Frost sidestepped.

It was a fountain, concrete or stone—he didn't know which.

He started to edge away from it, then stopped, the Arab swinging his sword.

Frost ducked, edging away from the blade and toward the fountain, feigning to stumble beside the lip of the dish-shaped bottom of the fountain. The harem guard swung and Frost dodged, slashing with his sword as the Arab's blade smashed against the lip of the fountain. Frost's blade sliced hard into the Arab's right thigh, the big man howling in agony, turning and hacking wildly with his sword.

Frost was on his feet again, edging toward the Canaretti girl and Julie Pulman.

The guard swung the blade again, Frost countering the swing, the blades locking. The big man, his right thigh streaming blood, was laughing. Frost smashed up with his right knee, going for the man's testicles. He impacted and nothing happened.

From behind him, like the voice of his conscience, he heard the Canaretti girl shout, "They're all eunuchs."

"Now you tell me?" Frost shouted back.

He fell back, the big man slicing down with the sword and Frost rolled. On his feet again, he remembered an old movie and reached to his left side. He released the keeper on the bayonet there.

As the big Arab swung his blade again, Frost dodged back, then swung his own blade, the two blades locking. Faces inches apart, the big man laughed again. Frost released his left hand from the sword's hilt, snatched at the bayonet on his left side and hammered it forward and upward, the blade impacting, Frost's left wrist nearly breaking.

The laugh on the big harem guard's face froze, then died there, the man toppling forward as Frost edged back.

"I'm glad people use guns these days," he sighed heavily. He dropped the sword from his shaking right hand, reloading the H-K pistol as he ran toward the Canaretti girl and Julie Pulman.

Chapter Thirteen

"Just who the hell are you anyway? My father sent you, right? The old—"

"Yeah," Frost told her, not bothering with her now. He leaned over Julie Pulman. "What—they got her drugged?"

"Sedated," the Canaretti girl answered, her voice sounding more subdued. "She was working with you?"

"Yeah. What's the difference between drugged and sedated?"

"Sedated—like after an operation."

Frost looked at the Canaretti girl, his eye riveting on her eyes. "What operation?"

"Ali Hassan Foudani—he was beating one of the other women, and Julie tried stopping him. She lost her temper I guess. She called him a coward to beat a woman. He had her tongue cut out. There wasn't anything I—" The girl looked away, leaving the sentence unfinished.

The automatic weapons fire outside was

more intense now, the explosions sounding nearer. The screaming had subsided since most of the women of the harem had fled.

"Cut out her tongue? Jesus . . . oh God!" Frost bent his head, looking at the Pulman girl, her face looking so placid under the sedation, the mouth closed—forever, in a way, he realized.

"Hey—you taking us out of here, or what? He'll do worse to her and me—and to you too."

Frost looked at the Canaretti woman. "Yeah—yeah, I'll take you out of here. But—" His throat was starting to tighten up, and the one-eyed man sniffed loudly as he swept Julie Pulman up into his arms. "That son of a—"

"Look out!"

Frost wheeled, clumsily with the Pulman woman in his arms, swinging the H-K on line, a single guard streaking toward them. "Eat lead, sucker," Frost growled, pumping two shots into the man, bowling him over as the Arab's hands went up to his face wounds as the body crumpled backwards.

"Yeah—let's get out of here," Frost said, his voice hoarse.

- Frost reached down and tried to snatch up the guard's Beretta. "Here, let me," the Canaretti girl said, getting the gun.

"Pick up any more souvenirs you can," he told her. "You know how to use a gun?"

"Am I my father's daughter?" Laughing, tears coming to her eyes, Frost's face softened.

"Okay, kid—let's give 'em hell!"

Frost started walking as fast as he could carry-

118

ing Julie Pulman. She was almost his own height—at least with shoes on—and she wasn't as light as she looked, he decided.

He glanced at the Canaretti girl, thinking she looked ridiculous in the pajama-like harem outfit with a gun in her hand. "What's the closest way to the side gate of the palace?"

"That way." The girl gestured toward a wooden double door on the far wall.

"Okay Miss Canaretti—let's boogie," he told her.

"Cut the Miss business. My friends call me Louie—and Mister whatever your name is, this qualifies you as a friend."

Despite himself, Frost almost laughed at her, the girl running ahead, snatching up three more pistols and one of the swords as she raced toward the double doors.

Frost, moving as quickly as he could with the unconscious Julie Pulman in his arms, followed after her, already anticipating that if his luck ran as it had been, the doors would be locked. The Canaretti girl was already wrestling the handles by the time Frost reached the doors.

"They're locked!"

Frost shook his head, taking the Pulman girl down from his arms, standing her limp body up as best he could and slinging her over his shoulder. He transferred the H-K pistol to his left hand, then took one of the Berettas from the Canaretti girl. "Don't you know that's what they make guns for?" Frost asked her, snubbing the front sight on his jeans pocket, then against

119

his belt when it slipped, working the slide back one-handedly—a dangerous practice since if the gun went off it could shoot him through the leg—and chambering the top round in the magazine. He told Louise, "All right—get back." Frost levelled the Beretta at the center of the two doors, between the door handles, firing once, then again, then a third time. "Hold me up so I don't lose my balance—get behind me," he rasped with Louise standing behind him, Frost leaned back against her, then kicked out with his right foot, almost losing his balance anyway despite the girl behind him as the door crashed open.

He emptied the Beretta into the hallway toward two more of the big guards. One of the shots hit low, and one man screamed, holding himself at the groin. "Mustn't have been a Eunuch—that one," Frost observed, stepping through the doorway, the Canaretti girl beside him. "Which way now?"

The girl looked up and down the T-shaped hallway, then pointed, "That way!"

"Okay, let's go," and Frost, the Pulman girl over his left shoulder, began to run, the H-K in his left fist, the borrowed Beretta in his right. There were several more—he stopped counting at six—of the guards coming toward them from the end of the hall and Frost began to fire. Hearing a gunshot from beside him, Frost saw Louise holding the Beretta outstretched in one hand, like a rimfire target shooter would at a competition, her feet squared apart in a boxer's stance. The gun belched fire again as he looked at her. Frost looked back up the hallway, and saw two of the men going down. There was more gunfire from the three or four men they hadn't yet gotten.

"Keep going," Frost told the woman, realizing suddenly that in a very different way than he, she was fighting for her life. If they'd cut Julie's tongue out for calling the Sheik a coward, he could imagine—but didn't want to—what they would do to the Canaretti girl for firing at harem guards aiding an escape.

He shook his head, and as he ran forward, the Beretta was outstretched ahead of him, punching deathpills toward the guards. The men were falling, and some of them were shooting back. Others charged with their swords twirling in the air, curses on their lips, their glistening half-naked bodies hurtling like juggernauts along the corridor, then stopped, slammed back by the tiny projectiles the pistols fired.

Frost and the Canaretti woman reached the end of the hallway, the Beretta in Frost's right hand empty, useless. Louise gave him another from one of the dead guards, working the slide for him, one gun in each of her hands now.

"I see why my dad liked the mob—this is terrific!" she enthused.

Frost just looked at her, incredulous. "Right, sure. Come on!" He stopped. "Which way?" he asked, but his ears already told him and as the girl pointed for him he was already running toward the sound of the gunfire and explosions.

Ahead of him, Frost could already see a wall of guards, and men in uniform as well, regular army troops of Akaran. The men formed a ragged defensive line, and beyond them, Frost could see his own men—some of them at least—fighting forward.

Frost skidded to a halt on his heels. He looked at Louie Canaretti. "Hey, Louie. You ever play football?"

"Yeah. Why?"

"I never did, but they tell me we gotta punch through their line—but we're all the ball. You ready?"

The girl looked down into her hands, at the cocked 9mms there. "Yeah—let's smoke those suckers!"

"Gotcha!" Frost, shouting all the dirty words he could think of at the top of his lungs, started running, holding onto Julie, shooting into the backs of the Sheik's defensive force as he and the girl headed down the corridor. Some of the troopers and palace guards were already turning, starting to return fire, but as they did, Frost heard and saw a grenade explosion. Then there was another. Frost saw his men starting to punch through from the other side of the sheik's defenders. Now all he had to do, Frost thought, was fight his way to link up with them—and stay alive in the process.

He fired out the Beretta in his right hand, and

as a guard stormed toward him, despite the burden of the Pulman girl on his shoulder, he dodged left, punching the pistol forward, ramming the slightly protruding muzzle of the big military 9mm autoloader into the face of the guard. The man shrieked a scream, throwing his hands to his face. Frost snatched the bayonet from the sheath on his right hip, then rammed it forward into the big guard's guts, drawing it out, slashing with the knife at a second guard, opening an artery or something—he wasn't looking closely enough to be sure—in the man's neck. Then he thrust the knife forward, leaving it in the chest of a third guard.

Frost shifted the H-K autoloader into his right hand, firing it twice, two of the subsonic 9mm hollow points pumping into the chest of another guard. He was about to shoot again, but stayed himself—it was Gilder. "Thank God man—come on—let me take the woman."

Frost, exhausted under the burden of the extra weight, helped Gilder get the woman onto his shoulder. Then Frost took Gilder's M-16 and the bandolier of spare magazines. Turning the M-16 into the hallway, Frost's trigger finger pumped three-round bursts. The Pulman girl's tongue was cut out and he was enjoying the killing and suddenly all he could hear was his own gun firing. Then Miles' hand was on his arm, the harem-outfitted Canaretti woman on his other side.

The girl said, "You beat them. They're dead."

Frost looked down the hallway—there would

be more troops coming, but these were dead. It was time to run. Frost looked at the Canaretti girl. "There's one I didn't get. I won't get him tonight either, maybe not this year, maybe not next. But he's dead—just as good as." Then Frost shouted to the hallway filled with dead men, the hallway that in another instant would be filled with soldiers after his blood, he knew. "You hear that, you bastard, Ali Hassan Foudani! You're as good as dead, you mother—"

Chapter Fourteen

The truck—mercifully, Frost reflected—was
still there. It was the truck they'd stolen earlier
that day, the provisions still loaded aboard.
They ditched the Travelall, blowing it up to
make it appear that either some of the raiders of
the harem had been killed, or that something
had somehow gone wrong. Hopefully, the
Sheik's men were looking in the opposite direction for Frost, the women and the mercenaries—
the ones left.

The ones left . . . Frost sat in the back of the
truck, the Canaretti woman's head on his left
shoulder, his eye riveted to the shadowy form of
the still sedated Julie Pulman on the floor of the
truck bed. Luciano had bought it, falling on a
grenade and saving Bohls and Smith. Then
Bohls had bought it, an assault rifle burst in the
face, half severing the top of his head from the
rest of his body. Sunshine Smith had stopped
three bullets in the left leg, then another slug in

his right arm—but according to Gilder, Smith would make it unless he got a bad infection.

Cohn had gotten wounded in the left hand, but the bleeding had stopped by now and he had told everyone the hand didn't hurt badly. Caldwell Miles, the stunt man, was unscathed—but there was a look in his eyes, and Frost thought if he had a mirror he'd see the look in his own eye. Too much death, too much for even a man who'd seen a lot of death to stand. Frost had no idea how many guards had been killed. He had killed several, and what worried him was that toward the end he had enjoyed it.

Frost wanted the Sheik—Ali Hassan Foudani—and until he exorcised that ghost he'd never be the same. It wasn't some kind of kid threat, Frost determined—he wasn't promising himself to cut the guy's tongue out. None of the poetic justice crap, Frost thought. He was just going to kill the man—the most expedient, the most definite way possible. That would be it.

Frost could break a promise to almost anyone if he had to—but not to himself, and not this. And the promise, too, was to the sleeping girl—Julie Pulman.

They travelled through the night, across the desert, blotting out their tracks as best as possible by an improved system based on the earlier "towel patrol" idea. They reached their safe sight for the day's camp—a high, rocky plateau housing a long-abandoned village. With the truck hidden in some of the building rubble and themselves interspersed throughout three of the buildings, there was relative safety, even from an air search.

Despite the early hour, Frost sat cross-legged on the dirt floor of one of the houses and searched in one of the packs. He found what he wanted: a bottle of whiskey. He opened the bottle, stared at it, then raised the bottle to his lips, taking a healthy-sized swallow, and leaning back on his elbow.

There was a hole in the building roof and through it he could watch the blueness of the sky without being subjected to the heat of the morning sun. He stayed there, alone, thinking. The Pulman girl was still resting, sedated, but her pulse was strong.

Maurice Gilder had examined and determined the Canaretti girl had not exaggerated—the tongue had been neatly cut out. Louise Canaretti had explained the Sheik had ordered the court physician to do it so it would be done properly. Frost took another drink of the whiskey, then leaned back again. Julie was resting and the Canaretti girl was changing into some of the clothes Julie had thought to bring for her. The rest of Frost's mercenaries were either resting or on guard. Gilder and Miles had volunteered to take their turn first since they were the fittest and the injured men needed the rest.

Frost looked at the bottle again. "Damnit!" He closed the bottle, tightening the cap so the contents wouldn't spill later. He continued to stare at the hole in the roof and the sky above it.

127

He lit a cigarette, turning, startled, as someone came into the small house.

It was Louise Canaretti, but he almost didn't recognize her. The harem girl outfit was replaced with a pair of khaki-colored slacks, and a long-sleeved shirt with the sleeves rolled above her elbows. The harem sandals were gone, too, replaced with a pair of dark brown, low rise boots.

"How are you doing, Hank?"

"Just terrific, Louie," Frost told her, dragging heavily on the cigarette.

"Give me a smoke, will ya?"

"Sure. Here." Frost tossed the girl the pack and his light. Nodding a thanks, she took one of the Camels, lit it, inhaled and held the smoke in her lungs for what seemed to Frost a long time.

She sat down, cross-legged on the floor, handing him back the cigarettes and the Zippo. "So, my father hired you guys. I knew he wouldn't just let me sit there. How much he payin' you?"

"A quarter of a million bucks. It wasn't worth it—no offense."

"Oh—hey, listen. I know what you mean. You're a gutsy guy, you know that?"

"Thanks—I guess," Frost told her.

"What you doin' about that other thing?"

"I'll get the Sheik—don't worry. I don't know when, but—"

"I don't mean the revenge trip."

"What are you talking about?" Frost asked the girl, the whiskey on his empty stomach

128

making him sleepy, but he was almost afraid to sleep, that he'd dream about what had happened to Julie Pulman.

"I mean those damned Nazis. They work for the Sheik—I overheard them. They're planning to knock off the—"

Frost sat bolt upright, hearing a shot, getting to his feet, half-running, half stumbling through the door of the small building, into the dusty town square. The M-16 was in his right hand by the carrying handle. The wind was blowing hard across the open plateau and sand stung his face as he scanned the open area. He saw nothing. Then, he heard Gilder shout, "Down here—my God!"

Frost bent into a low, loping run, the M-16 at a high port as he started toward the building where they had left Julie Pulman.

He reached the entranceway, saw Maurice Gilder backing out and watched as Gilder turned around. A thought flashed across Frost's mind—people who have never worked closely or spent time with black people might find it difficult to recognize someone who was black as being pale. The skin gets a grayish tinge, especially around the cheeks. Gilder looked like that. Gilder was talking then, "She must have snatched the thing earlier—it's one of the pistols we grabbed at the palace. I—mother of God." Gilder turned quickly around the corner of the building and Frost could hear the sounds of the man vomiting.

Frost, pushed the Canaretti girl back behind

him, saying, "Stay outside." He stepped through the doorway. There was no hole in the roof here, and so the light was poorer. He was grateful for that.

Julie Pulman lay sprawled on the floor of the hut, the big, military autoloading pistol on the floor near her right hand. He picked up the gun—the slide was locked back. She'd been a pro all the way, Frost thought. To avoid an accidental discharge injuring someone else when the gun fell from her hand in death, she'd stripped the magazine and had only one cartridge in the chamber. There wasn't too much left of her face or the top of her head . . . Frost started to feel sick.

He dropped to the dirty floor. On the floor, written neatly—apparently with her finger as the writing instrument scrawling into the dirt—was a note or message. "Hank Frost, you did good. Thank you, for me, for everything. Don't forget to get the Canaretti girl out—don't waste it all. This was my only choice. Love, Julie."

Frost stripped off the blanket on the cot they set up, covering the girl with it, then walked out of the hut. Louise Canaretti was standing beside the entrance. "I'm going to let Gilder and the others get you out—I've got work to do," Frost began, lighting another cigarette.

"You're damned right you got work," the girl began with her New York accent showing loud and clear. "The Nazi guys working for that damned Sheik. You know who they're planning to knock off?"

"I don't care—let 'em knock each other off," Frost started.

"Well, you better care. The Sheik—he's one of those Moslem fanatics, the kind that hates America, hates any moderate Arab leader, hates Israel, hates everybody who isn't a Moslem fanatic practically. Well—"

"I don't care," Frost almost shouted.

"Well, you better. If they make their lousy hit, there could be World War Three. I overheard the whole thing—figured it might help me later to know what was going on."

"So what!"

The Canaretti girl punched Frost in the stomach and he turned and glared at her. "They got two little Nazi crumbums workin' with 'em that are gonna dress up like Israeli commandos, then they're gonna knock off the President of Egypt and blame the Jews. You better damn well care!"

Frost looked at the woman. It was like a bad dream, the whole thing. The plan going sour, the thing they did to Julie Pulman, now her suicide, the Nazis too now, going after the President of Egypt.

"Did you hear me?" The girl was screaming, and Frost guessed part of it was because she knew what was inside the hut behind him.

"Yeah, I heard you," Frost said, his voice calm, all of the whiskey that had eaten at his guts burned away. "I heard you real good. I saw them rehearsing but didn't know who they wanted to kill. Where's it going to be—when?"

"I don't know that. One of those damned harem guards was coming. I got my butt whipped for being where I wasn't supposed to be anyway."

His voice sounded lifeless to him, when he said, "They had some kind of speaker's platform mock-up set up out there in the desert, some funny kinds of statues and stuff."

"Take me there—I minored in archeology. Maybe I can peg it. Maybe it's some kind of tomb site."

"What happens if we get caught—you get caught?"

"You really want to know?"

Frost looked at her and nodded, thinking almost absently that she sounded like somebody out of a detective novel, not a Ph.D. in paleontology.

"Well," she said, thoughtfully. "I'd do like I guess Julie did in there—the Dutch act. That Ali Hassan Foudani is never gettin' his hands on me again."

"Okay," Frost said, suddenly tired, too tired to care. "I'll take you there, then we'll do what we can. We've gotta bury—"

"I'm goin' in there. If we're puttin' her in the ground, I think she'd want to be buried in something beside that harem outfit. You know?"

"Yeah, but, it's not—"

"It wasn't pretty when they made us watch them cut her tongue out either—for discipline they said, for our education they said. And Foudani was smilin'—that bastard!"

132

Frost walked away, the girl entering the hut. He heard a low gasp, but not a scream. If he'd been a woman, he thought, he would have screamed. It was that bad.

As he walked across the plateau, the wind lacing at him, a cigarette hanging dead in the left corner of his mouth, the M-16 muzzle back on his right shoulder and half across his neck, Frost muttered, "Foudani was smiling . . ."

Chapter Fifteen

They'd left Gilder and Miles with the Land Rover. Frost and the girl were walking toward the assassination practice sight, no one having said much of anything for the several hour long drive. Frost and the Canaretti girl were silent now as they walked.

Mentally, Frost reviewed the situation, occasionally staring up at the stars just to relieve the boredom. He was now a wanted criminal throughout the Moslem world. Despite Sheik Ali Hassan Foudani's rather disgusting personal habits and his right-wing Moslem, anti-American position, he was still very much respected politically. Foudani could clearly label the harem invasion as a violation of Moslem womanhood—and that would mean death for Frost almost anywhere in the Moslem world. Because of his own problem with that, and Foudani's respected position, it would be

impossible to go to any Moslem authorities—
even the Egyptian ones—and warn them of the
attempt to be made on the life of the Egyptian
President. To go to the Israelis would be possible, since the Israelis were known to distrust
and dislike Foudani. Although security might
be tightened around the target, Foudani would
not be arrested on the passed-along word of the
Israeli Mossad. At any event, if the assassination were close, it would take too much time for
the Egyptian authorities to investigate tactfully
what the Israelis could tell them if Frost could
convince them.

Almost bitterly, Frost realized he knew the
answer to the problem. If Foudani's assassins
were to be stopped, he would have to do it himself. Maybe with the help of his mercenary team,
maybe with the Canaretti girl helping out. But
it would all devolve to him—Hank Frost.

"What'd you say?" the girl asked him.

"Not a thing. The desert wind is playing
tricks on your ears," he told her. "It was just
over that ridge there, in the valley beyond it."

"Right," the girl said, starting to walk a little
faster.

"Hang on—we have to check out the valley
first. We don't want to walk into a reception
committee, or another practice session. Right?"

"Yeah," she agreed.

They stopped at the base of the ridge. Then
Frost and the girl moved slowly in the shifting
sand up toward the ridge top itself. Frost

dropped flat within a dozen feet of the top, pulling the girl down beside him, then crawling toward the top.

Frost peered over the side of the high dune and down into the valley. The stage was still set there, but the players were not in sight. "I think it's safe," he told the Canaretti girl. "Look for yourself. See if you can figure it—"

"Holy God," she half-screamed. "I know that place. See those statue-like things, and that facade behind the speaker's platform over there? That's in the Valley of the Kings. Just before those creeps snatched me, I was reading about it in some magazine. There was a temple site just partially restored. The President was going to speak there."

"Well—"

"What day is it?"

"What do you mean, what day is it?"

"They don't give you a damned calendar in the harem, all right!"

Frost glanced at his watch, telling her the date.

"God—that's four days from now—almost five. That's when they're doing it, when he's making his address at the temple restoration—something about the cultural heritage Egypt has given the world. Something that the Western world needs to be made more aware that Egypt's present greatness is inextricably tied to its past—"

"Perfect subject for them, too, isn't it?"

"Those crumbums! How do we stop 'em, Hank?"

Frost looked at the girl. "I was afraid you were going to ask that." He stared down into the rehearsal area, trying to memorize the details in his mind, somehow knowing he would need to remember every possible piece of the stage, every movement the players he'd watched would make. "Okay—we gotta get out of Akaran. We're hamstrung until we do. Then, maybe Israeli security." Frost stopped, thinking. A name stuck in his mind, part of a name. He'd been working a detail years back, when he'd met some Egyptian security man and struck up a conversation. "What was his name?"

"Whose name?" the girl asked, sounding puzzled.

"This Egyptian security man I met once— long time ago. He struck me as real sensible, knew his stuff, too. Tough guy, smart—what the heck was his—" Frost stopped.

It was the graying mustache, the full shock of hair, flecked with gray, the black eyes—he remembered the man now. About ten years older than Frost was. Shariff Abdusalem. He was with the Egyptian Secret Service. Frost couldn't remember the proper name of the outfit.

"Shariff Abdusalem—"

"Does it hurt?" the girl cracked.

"No—" Frost was suddenly irritated. "No, that's the guy's name, the guy I know. If I can

137

reach him, if he remembers me so he doesn't think I'm some crackpot, maybe we've got a chance. Maybe—come on. Seen enough?"

The girl only nodded.

Frost started sliding back down the ridge. He'd seen enough, years and years of enough.

Chapter Sixteen

Frost had determined there was nothing Gilder and the others could do to help. With phoney identification papers, then ditching their guns before crossing the border, they could make it into Egypt and out of the country. It was his face and the girl's face the authorities would be looking for. Because of that, Frost had given the mercenaries the Land Rover and he and the girl, now a day's drive into the desert, were using the truck. The truck was more likely to be spotted than the Rover as being involved in the raid on the Harem. Frost had decided on the original escape route Julie Pulman had set up through the Greek arms dealer. On the far border of Akaran, each day there would be a helicopter that would land and wait for ten minutes, then fly off. All Frost and the girl had to do was reach the spot and hope the helicopter was still keeping to the schedule.

Gilder and the others had not wanted to leave

Frost and the girl alone, reasoning that if they encountered a desert patrol of Ali Hassan Foudani's men, Frost with none of his men to help wouldn't stand a chance. Frost had insisted that splitting up was the only way and said nothing more about it.

If all went well, they would rendezvous on the island of Crete at the end of the second day or soon after that.

The desert heat stifled any desire to eat throughout the day. But when Frost and Louise Canaretti finally made their camp that night, Frost ate ravenously—despite the stale food. Not daring a fire, sitting in the shadow of the truck beyond a low ridge of dunes quite a distance off the road, the girl finally sat down beside him. He looked at her. Her face was clean, her hair combed. "Well," she said defensively. "You said we had plenty of water if I wanted to clean up a little. Well—"

"You look good, Louie—good," Frost smiled.

"What are you thinking about?"

"Everything, nothing. Don't worry about it."

"You saved my life, guy. I worry about you."

"Don't," Frost told her.

"What if I want to?"

"Your father wouldn't like it."

"What—you afraid if you touch me he'll put out a contract on you or somethin'?"

"Let me ask you a question," Frost began. "Now, I understand you went to all the best schools, were a real whiz—still are. How come you—"

"Talk like some broad off the corner, you mean?"

Frost shrugged, then, "Yeah—sort of."

"It's intentional—or at least it was. Now it's habit. See—I knew what my dad did all along. Kids learn more than grownups think they do. First I learned my father was a big guy in the Mob—a Capo, maybe even Capo de Tutti Capi, if you know what I mean. I never figured that out. But anyway, first when I learned, I was ashamed. I wanted to be anybody besides me. But then I started to figure. My mother loved my father a whole heap; I loved him too. He was always good to us, always did everythin' for us. Not just givin' us things, but bein' with us and everythin'. He was always there for me—you know?"

"No," Frost smiled, lighting a cigarette. "You were luckier than I was."

"I'm sorry—really. But—well, I figured that I wasn't plannin' on getting into the rackets— womens lib hasn't gotten that far yet—don't know if it ever will. It would have been the easiest thing in the world to change the way I talked, sound like the other girls I went to school with. Maybe I figured it was the only real link to my family, a way of showin' 'em I loved 'em and maybe more important, respected 'em. Does that sound dumb?"

"Maybe what you did sounds dumb," Frost answered thoughtfully, "but not the reason behind it. Naw—it isn't dumb, I guess."

"Hey, Hank?"

141

"Yeah—what?"

"It looks like you're never gonna ask, and maybe Julie bein' dead has somethin' to do with it. And don't think I'm one of them pushy dames—but you wanna sleep with me?"

"How'd your parents wind up with a blonde-haired, blue-eyed Italian kid?"

The girl laughed, the corners of her mouth crinkling when she did, making something like dimples, Frost thought.

"Well—my mother was Italian, really—but her father, he was Swiss. I guess I'm some kind of throwback, you know?"

"Throwback, huh," Frost echoed. "Okay. Sounds all right." Frost put his left arm around the girl, drawing her near him. He looked at her closely. "You sure?"

"Yeah—it's not just the gratitude thing for savin' my life—I kinda like ya."

"You are crazy, kid," Frost told her, kissing her hard on the mouth as he felt her hands and arms around his neck. Moving his hands across her body, feeling her respond to him, hearing her breathing against him, Frost realized how badly he had wanted something to take his mind away from the whole thing of what had happened, to make him feel alive inside again. He kissed her so hard she screamed a little, but then only held him more tightly . . .

Chapter Seventeen

Frost had left the road when they'd started again that morning, deciding that the nearer they drew to the border the more chance there was of encountering a patrol of the Sheik's men. Leaving the road made it doubly slow going, for each time they started over a high ridge, Frost would get out, checking that they weren't driving into a trap. After a while—he guessed the exhaustion was showing—the girl volunteered to do some of the running and finally, after three more ridge lines, he let her. At least she could handle a gun, he knew.

Frost figured there remained another ten miles to the border as he sat in the truck cab, the engine idling and giving off more heat than he wanted to think about. He checked his watch. If they could make it without any problems across the remaining miles, they'd be just about on time for the scheduled helicopter landing. He was about to shout to the girl as she scrambled up the dune, to tell her to hurry, but he knew she was tired, more exhausted than she let on.

Instead, he bided his time. He lit a cigarette, and checked the Omega again. He checked the H-K P7, the silencer and the special slide replaced by the standard slide, the little 9mm in the shoulder holster provided for it under his left arm. He had given the girl the G.I. shoulder rig and the .45 so she'd be armed at all times. He understood her desire that if capture seemed imminent, she would kill herself. But he'd already promised himself that if capture seemed imminent, he would kill her before she could do it to herself. She was Catholic and suicide was a sin, he remembered. No sense, he'd told himself, letting her go out with something like that on her conscience.

He looked up, seeing the girl running, slipping, then sliding down the dune, waving her arms frantically. He started to climb out of the truck cab, to shout to her that she was acting crazy.

Then, as she reached the bottom of the dune, he saw the look in her eyes. He looked behind her, hearing something—the sound of a motor, then another and another, too loud to be far away. He threw the truck into gear, releasing the brake and letting out the clutch, starting it rumbling toward her, then looked to the top of the dune ridge again. There was a man running over the top of the dune, the uniform that of Sheik Ali Hassan Foudani's desert patrol force, a Soviet AK-47 assault rifle in his hands.

"Damn!" Frost rasped, cutting the wheel of the truck in a sharp right toward the girl, with his right hand snatching the H-K pistol and squeeze-cocking it as he gripped the 9mm in his fist, thrusting the gun outside the cab window and pumping off two fast shots. He guessed both of them connected as the soldier seemed lifted up off his feet, then crashed back over onto the far side of the dune, disappearing from sight.

The girl was screaming, "Hank! They're coming—a dozen or so Land Rovers and bunches of guys like him!"

Frost dropped the pistol on the seat beside him. "Shut up and get aboard," Frost hollered, cutting the wheel sharply to the right. The truck teetered on the edge of rolling over, but stayed upright.

The girl was running toward him and he slowed, waving her in front of the vehicle, slowing still more as she ran alongside him now, clamboring up onto the running board. Her face was in the window and she shouted, "Okay—I'm okay!"

As she started in through the doorway, Frost hit the gas hard, looking to his left and behind him, seeing the lead Land Rovers starting over the ridge, some of them already beginning to turn after him. Glancing back to his right, seeing the girl in her seat beside him, he stomped on the clutch, upshifting into second. Then he shifted again, into third this time—he couldn't risk going into a higher gear than that because of the poor traction on the sand.

"What do I do?" the girl shouted.

"Take a gun and start shooting at 'em. What the hell do you think you should do?"

Frost cut the wheel right again, the Land Rovers still coming over the ridge in a long, ragged line. Some of them were as close as twenty yards. A machine gun, mounted on the back of one of them toward the middle of the formation, started firing.

The girl was shooting too, now, one of the two M-16s they'd kept. She was firing but not doing any visible damage to their pursuers that Frost could detect. He cut the wheel sharp to the left as the machine gun opened up again. He counted twelve Land Rovers and three times that many men, some of them on foot, firing assault rifles, some of them standing in the backs of the vehicles, shooting submachine guns.

The machine gunner was opening up again, the sand rippling beside the truck under the impact of the bullets. Frost cut the wheel right—they were trying to prevent him from getting across the ridge, he realized. Perhaps he was closer to the border than he'd thought. He wheeled the truck hard right, then another hard right, cutting a big swath in the white sand. One of the Rovers impacted against the rear of the truck, upending, the men riding it spilling out.

Frost downshifted into first, skipping second altogether, starting for the dune ridge. He went into the middle of the line of Rovers, the truck's massive front bumper smashing hard into another of the vehicles, pushing it along the sand, then overturning it and rolling it aside. The machine gun was opening up again and Frost, tucking down behind the wheel, shouted to the girl, "Get down! Look—" The windshield shattered, glass spraying over Frost's hands and bare arms and all across the seat. He silently thanked God he was wearing his sunglasses rather than just the eyepatch with nothing protecting his good right eye. He realized in that instant that he'd become paranoid about the loss of his right eye—about blindness.

He upshifted into second, the truck getting stuck as it started to climb the dune. There were two Rovers immediately behind him now. Partly to get the truck unstuck, partly to knock the vehicles out, Frost stomped hard on the clutch, effectively putting the truck's transmission into neutral. The massive vehicle rolled back. He couldn't see it, but he could hear the truck crunching into the two Land Rovers. Frost punched forward on the stick, getting the transmission into first. The truck lurched forward, a ripping, tearing sound from behind him. The Rover with the machine gun was opening up again and Frost cut the wheel into a hard right, taking off laterally and upward across the dune ridge toward the top. He heard the machine gun bullets whizzing and pinging along the side of the truck and hoped they didn't hit the engine or the radiator or the gas tank. He stomped down on the clutch, trying again for second gear, the truck lurching ahead.

The girl beside him was shooting again, and as he cut the wheel, the truck slipping down in the sand, trying to get it aimed toward the top of the ridge, he could see two men in one of the Rovers behind them getting cut down. "Good girl!" he shouted over the wind of the slipstream, the engine and transmission noise, the gunfire.

"Thanks a bunch, Hank," the girl shouted back, firing again.

"Go for that machine gunner—try to disable the Rover if you can!"

"Gotcha, man!" The girl swapped magazines in the M-16 and began to fire again.

They were nearing the top of the ridge line and the truck wasn't making it. Frost downshifted into first, the truck slowing, then seeming to lurch ahead with the lower gear giving it the power the engine needed. The truck bounced over the ridge line and over the side. Frost fought the wheel, trying to keep the truck from toppling over, getting it going along the ridge line toward the valley on the other side at its base.

He could see one of the Land Rovers, bouncing over the ridge line, the girl's M-16 firing, the Rover not slowing. If anything, it was speeding up, sailing away from the ridge line. Something Louise had hit made the thing explode in mid-air. Then the vehicle came crashing down along the dune, rolling—still on fire—down toward the valley.

Frost upshifted into second, then into third, the truck seeming to race under him along the side of the ridge, the valley floor now less than two hundred yards away.

Something—he didn't quite know what—made him glance at the Omega on his left wrist as he cut the wheel past his line of sight. There were five minutes until the chopper would be landing, maybe less than that if the watch were a little off or the chopper pilot a little early.

Frost downshifted into second as the truck bounced over a hummock, coming down hard into the valley floor. He upshifted into third, the sand more hard-packed here, then into fourth, starting to move away from the Rovers. The sideview mirror shattered as the Rover with the machine gun mounted on the back rolled across the dune ridge, the machine gun firing in long bursts.

"Get down. That sucker's shooting at us again," Frost shouted to the girl.

"Hang on, Hank!" The girl, Frost glancing toward her, fired a long burst with the M-16. Frost craned his neck to look behind the truck again. The Land Rover with the machine gun on it had come to a dead halt in the sand, the windshield visibly shot out, the machine gun silenced.

"You can be on my team anytime, girl," Frost shouted to her. One of the Land Rovers was pulling up alongside them now and Frost fumbled on the seat among the shards of broken glass, finding the H-K 9mm. This time the gun

149

was loaded with standard 9mm ammo scarfed from some of the captured pistols of the palace guards. He fired the H-K across his body and down into the seat of the Land Rover, the vehicle swerving, dropping back. Frost cut the wheel in a sharp left, then right, swatting at the Rover with the rear end of the truck.

"You got it!" the girl almost squealed, shouting, screaming her enthusiasm.

"Nuts!" Frost muttered, thinking about the girl. He dropped the pistol on the seat again, in the distance his eye catching something that he hoped wasn't a mirage, but a helicopter instead.

Frost cut the wheel left, aiming the truck toward what he had seen, hoping the helicopter—if indeed it really were a helicopter—wouldn't get frightened off by the gunfire. If this were the border, and if it were the right chopper, he had no illusions that crossing an imaginary line would end the pursuit by the Sheik's troops.

He stomped down hard on the gas, shouting to the girl, "Hang on kid—that's the chopper up ahead!" Now, indeed, he was certain of it, certain the machine was the one waiting for them, that the border was perhaps five hundred yards away.

There was a Rover coming up along on the driver's side of the truck and Frost cut the wheel sharp to the left, trying to nail it. But the Rover edged away, untouched.

"Look out!" the girl shouted, Frost turning, seeing her waving the muzzle of the M-16 toward his face.

"What are you doing?"

"Smokin' that crumbum—what d'ya think?"

Before Frost could say anything, the girl had the rifle leveled just inches from his nose, and on his left he could see the Rover coming up again, a man in the back on his knees, holding a submachine gun, the gun already starting to chatter toward them. "Shoot already!" Frost shouted.

The girl shot, the fire at the muzzle seeming scorchingly hot as the bullets whizzed past his face, his head involuntarily snapping back. He glanced to his left—the man with the sub gun was dead or the next best thing to it. The Rover was out of control, the driver collapsed over the wheel, the man beside him fighting for a moment to grab the wheel, to get the vehicle under control. As the Rover hit a hummock of hard-packed dirt, the passenger was jolted away and trapped in the rolling, exploding Rover.

Frost cut the truck's wheel right, straightening as he aimed the hood ornament toward the helicopter. The chopper seemed to be lifting off. He wanted to shout, "No—wait!" But it wouldn't have done any good. He stomped the gas pedal to the floor, leaving the five remaining Rovers behind for an instant. Glancing back again, he saw them coming up fast.

"Try and signal that chopper, Louie!"

The girl and Frost exchanged glances, then the girl started ripping off her blouse. Wearing nothing above her waist but her bra, she stuck her right arm out of the truck window and began waving the blouse.

"Wonderful," Frost rasped, but at the same time couldn't think of anything better to do. The chopper was a hundred yards away now, and he started downshifting, slowing the truck, cutting the wheel into a hard right. The chopper seemed to hover a few inches over the ground.

"Get ready to run," Frost shouted to the Canaretti girl, downshifting fast, the truck lurching to a halt. Frost jumped down from behind the wheel, the H-K pistol in his left hand, one of the M-16s in his right. He could see the girl, firing the assault rifle toward the fast advancing Rovers as she ran. He tried shouting to her, but could barely hear himself over the gunfire and the whirring of the helicopter's rotor blades.

He started to run, firing the handgun and the assault rifle as he ran.

The girl was twenty feet or so ahead of him, ducking now under the rotor blades.

Frost's guts froze—maybe it wasn't the chopper that was waiting for them, maybe—but there wasn't time to worry. As he hit the boundary under the rotor blades, sand blowing up around him as if in a dust storm, he wheeled, emptying the M-16 toward the Rovers, shattering the windshield of the lead vehicle, the Rover spinning out, a second Land Rover crashing into it.

Frost held the empty rifle in his right fist and

ran, diving for the chopper door as the big commercial machine started to lift off. Frost felt a set of hands reaching for him as he hauled his body inward.

He looked up, saw Louie, then saw the face belonging to the hands. "I am Mahmed, Captain Frost. I work for the Greek merchant— you recall?"

It was the man with the fez. Frost half felt like kissing him as the chopper pulled up and started across the desert.

Chapter Eighteen

Frost sat on a rough wooden folding chair, his feet propped up against a low stone fence. Far below him was the sea. They had been in the Greek merchant's house on Crete since midnight. He glanced at his watch—nine-thirty a.m. He had slept eight hours, but felt as though he hadn't slept at all.

After the helicopter ride across the desert, there had been a long, searingly hot car ride to the sea, then a ride in what Frost assumed was a lifeboat out to the seaplane, then the seaplane ride to Crete. There had been some anxious moments while the man with the fez— Mahmed—had explained their passports and visas—all of which were forged—to the immigration man in the hut along the pier. But nothing had come of it and there had been a short ride up toward the house. Frost had belted away two drinks, then rolled into bed, the Canaretti girl sleeping the night in his arms. His right arm was asleep when he'd awakened.

A cook came with the house and Frost had gotten her to make eggs and a small steak. He'd shown her how to make hash browned potatoes—they'd wound up "cottage fried" in the translation. Sipping at his sixth cup of coffee, his hair still wet from the shower, Frost stared down at the waves below. He was glad to be out alive.

Mahmed was in the town, verifying that Frost's mercenaries had gotten out of Egypt and were on the way. He was also trying to run down a lead that would provide a way of reaching Shariff Abdusalem, the Egyptian Secret Intelligence Service Agent Frost needed so desperately to contact if anything were to be done to stop the assassination.

He looked at the date on his watch face. There remained less than three days if the girl—who'd gone back to sleep now—had remembered the date in the article properly. On this too, Mahmed—an invaluable fellow, Frost decided—was checking. He had remarked that there was a man at one of the wire services who could help him.

Frost finished the coffee and set the cup on the stones beside him, lighting a cigarette. He turned the battered Zippo over in his hand, looking at it. The finish wasn't something to jump up and down about, he thought, but it had held up well through saltwater swims, dust storms, freezing temperatures. And the lighter worked—he liked things that worked, thinking perhaps that sometimes that was the only thing he liked about himself.

"Captain Frost—Captain!"

Frost turned to his left and started to get up when he saw Mahmed coming at a brisk pace up from the driveway along the narrow stone steps.

Frost turned around in the chair instead, swinging his legs down. He was still tired. "You found something out, Mahmed?"

"It is," the man huffed and puffed, "as you and the young woman said. The President of Egypt makes an address late in the afternoon the day following tomorrow, in the Valley of the Kings. Your men—they will arrive here in Crete in three days and are already safely aboard a steamer which will come here by a circuitous route. I will meet them in the event of your absence."

"And what about a way of contacting—"

The man with the fez cut him off. "This, too, has been done. The Egyptian, Shariff Abdu-salem—I have located the office through which he works. It may be the fortunes of Allah which guide me in this endeavor, and now only if he will be at his office when you call we shall all be rewarded."

Frost looked at the man, liking him, but not quite really understanding him all the time. "Then you got his phone number?"

"Yes, that is correct, Captain Frost."

"Gimme," Frost said, starting to his feet, "and then point me in the direction of a telephone. And keep your fingers crossed too, pal."

156

Frost took the neatly folded piece of paper, read the number and wondered absently if he could dial direct, then shook his head.

The wait for the connection seemed interminable to Frost, the air inside the house stifling by comparison to the fresh sea air of the veranda. There were whirring, clicking, computer-like sounds—everything except a ringing. Then suddenly the connection was made. Frost wondered what he would say. He decided on the direct approach.

A man answered, identifying the number as belonging to a rug vending firm. Frost was sick of fake rug vendors. "My name is Frost. I want to talk with one of your—ahh, salesmen, Shariff Abdusalem. He and I met several years ago at a—rug security conference. The head of your rug company—the President, as a matter of fact—is in extreme danger and I can save him from this. But I must speak with Abdusalem. Tell him it is the man with the eyepatch he met in Geneva—the one who told the jokes. I'll wait."

The man on the other end of the line grunted something and the connection seemed to go dead. Frost hoped instead he was on hold. Several minutes passed, and as Frost nearly decided the connection really was dead, the line suddenly came alive again.

"This is Shariff Abdusalem," the deep, sleepy sounding voice on the other end of the line announced with an air of finality.

"Shariff? This is Hank Frost—remember—"

"I remembered the jokes, my friend. I understand you have had some difficulty recently in one of our neighboring countries. You are wishing, perhaps, to turn in yourself?"

"That's turn yourself in—not turn in yourself," Frost corrected automatically. "No—I didn't do anything wrong. I'll tell you about it later. How freely can we talk?"

"Not terribly," Abdusalem said after a moment.

"You know who I mean by the President of the rug company? Did the other guy tell you?" Frost asked.

"He mentioned your rather peculiar remarks. I assume I know to whom you refer. Trouble for him?"

"The kind we were trying to protect against when we met in Geneva. Very serious trouble, if we don't act before the day after tomorrow in the afternoon—at the Val—"

"I know the place of which you speak. Where shall we meet?"

Frost's mind raced. "How fast can I get to Tel-Aviv from Crete?"

There was silence for a moment. "Neutral ground, eh? Very well—you can likely make it by this evening. I will be in the bar all night at my hotel," and he gave Frost the name.

"I know it," Frost told him.

"Very well—until tonight." The line clicked dead. Frost assumed Abdusalem would by now be starting to bark the initial orders to check into any possible threats against the President, have the security checked out. Frost counted the Egyptian agent as one of the most efficient people he'd ever met—despite the sleepy sounding voice. Frost hoped he was right.

"Mahmed," he shouted. "Get me to Tel-Aviv. I need to be there by tonight." Frost started up the stairs toward the bedroom to wake the Canaretti girl. Kiss off another night's sleep, he thought.

Chapter Nineteen

Frost had always liked Tel-Aviv, and now he especially liked it. If there were any place outside the United States safe from the men of Sheik Ali Hassan Foudani, it was Israel. There was an ancillary disadvantage which made him uncomfortable. He was weaponless again, but it couldn't be helped.

Frost had registered in the same hotel, using another forged set of papers for himself and Louise Canaretti, these almost cheerfully and ridiculously quickly provided by Mahmed. He was a handy man to have around indeed, Frost thought again. As Mr. and Mrs. Howard Straburg, Frost and the girl came down the steps from their room—Frost didn't like elevators after a bad experience once—and started across the lobby toward the bar. He hadn't tried sneaking a look at the old-fashioned book-style hotel register to see if Abdusalem had signed into the hotel under his own name—but he doubted that it mattered.

The bar was crowded, built to look like any bar from Manhattan to Singapore or anywhere in between, with its panelled walls, subdued lighting, and air conditioning to clean smoke from the air. Frost shrugged, starting the girl across the room and up three low steps. They went past a mezzanine with small two-seater tables, but these were too crowded. They walked toward some larger booths dominating the far wall. Frost automatically assumed Abdusalem would have commandeered one of these. It would be the only place with at least a modicum of privacy.

And Frost stopped, his hand squeezing the Canaretti girl's left elbow a moment. She looked at him and Frost murmured, "There he is—over there," then started toward the end booth. Frost stopped beside the table, the Egyptian agent looking up across a martini. "You look just like I remember you looking—ten years older than I am."

"And you, my friend, are just as I remember you. I would describe my memory in greater detail except for the presence of the lady." Abdusalem, stood, extending his hand to Frost, then looking at Louise Canaretti.

"This is Louie," Frost told Abdusalem.

"Louie—what a perfectly charming name. I am called Shariff by my friends. Please—why don't we all sit down and perhaps order a drink."

Frost let Louise Canaretti slide into the

horseshoe-shaped booth seat first so she'd be between Abdusalem and himself, then Frost sat down beside her. Abdusalem waved over a waiter, the girl ordering a gin & tonic and Frost—feeling in a medicinal mood—ordered a double scotch on the rocks. Abdusalem gestured toward his own drink and the waiter nodded.

"Moslems aren't supposed to drink—right?" Frost asked.

Abdusalem smiled. "Jews aren't supposed to do any work on the Sabbath, I understand too. It never seems to bother them if there's a military operation under way though—hmm?"

"You guys always talk like this?" Frost looked at the Canaretti girl, and so did the Egyptian, then all three of them began to laugh.

"You are a wanted man—but you know that, of course."

"It's good to be wanted," Frost told Abdusalem.

"Yes—how true. But not good to be captured, heh?"

"Are you guys ever gonna get to the point—or what?" Canaretti interjected.

"She's right, you know," Frost smiled. The drinks came, Frost sipping at his, grimacing, then adding, "Good scotch."

"You referred to some sort of problem for the President of my rug company. And what might that be?"

"You want to tell him?" Frost asked Louise Canaretti.

"No—no you tell him."

"Okay," Frost began, nodding. "You know," he said to Abdusalem, "about the harem thing. Well, Louise's father hired me to get her out. She was kidnapped by a gang of white slavers and sold to Ali Hassan Foudani. Her father also hired Julie Pulman—"

"The detective?"

"Yes—the late detective. Foudani had Julie's tongue cut out after she arranged for her own kidnapping to get herself into the harem and make contact with Louie, and then Julie killed herself because of what Foudani had done to her."

"That is singularly unfortunate," Abdusalem interjected. "For many reasons of course, but a person of such international reknown as Miss Pulman could certainly have added the proper ring of authenticity to your story. I had no idea Foudani would go to such lengths—it has been rumored, of course, that his morals are somewhat lacking, but one can never know," the Egyptian concluded, gesturing expansively with his hands.

"Well, Louie here overhead him plotting with a couple of guys—presumably Nazis of some kind. They are planning to kill—uh, the President of your rug company. Independently of her, along with some of my team I watched a rehearsal for the assassination. I showed Louie the sight after we got her out, and she pegged it as the Valley of the Kings. He's making an address there, your President—"

"I know. A close friend is in charge of the security."

"Yeah, but Foudani," the girl interrupted. "Well, he wants to start a war. The guys he got to make the hit—"

"The hit? Oh, yes—the hit."

"Yeah, those guys are gonna be dressed like Israeli soldiers, commandoes."

"So," Abdusalem said thoughtfully, "if our President is killed, or even if he is not, the Israelis will at least initially be blamed. And persons like Foudani who have always argued for all-out war with Israel will have their way perhaps."

"Question is—how can we stop it?" Frost lit a Camel with the Zippo, turning the lighter over in his hands.

"You did well to come to me with this. But why not the Israelis, or Interpol?"

"The Israelis were one possibility. But coming from outside Egypt, to get anything done would have taken too long. Going to you, I'm cutting out the middle man, so to speak. With Interpol, what could they do—launch an investigation? By the time it got started, especially with the kind of cooperation Foudani would give to investigating himself, well—" Frost let the idea hang.

"How certain are you that this information is accurate?"

"I heard," the girl insisted, emphatically poking her finger toward Abdusalem.

"Unless something has already happened or will happen to alter their plans, it's going to happen," Frost said flatly.

"What do you suggest I do?" Abdusalem asked, sipping at his fresh martini. "I have already, based on our rather scanty conversation by telephone, done what I can to heighten security measures. I can have my people searching for these Nazis when they enter the country. There are many small things I have already begun and many small things I can now undertake. But in light of what transpired at the harem, in light of who is bringing this information of a supposed assassination attempt, and that Foudani, an otherwise respected man, is behind it—well, it will be difficult. I cannot even entertain the hope of my President cancelling his address, nor can I do much to alter the physical security. We are already in the habit of well protecting our President, and Foudani would know this. There is little we can do to improve upon our usual measures. If they have planned this assassination as you insist, then they have planned to get around our usual security procedures."

"You're saying," Frost began, "there's not much we really can do, right?"

"Perhaps one thing. You and the woman have seen these men, and have seen the 'rehearsal arena,' if you will."

"If I set foot in a Moslem country and get recognized, I'm dead," Frost told the Egyptian.

"Not if you help to foil a plot to kill that Moslem country's president."

"What if we can't foil the plot, as you said?"

"I would do what I can to keep you from harm's way."

"Hell—" Frost stubbed out his cigarette and lit another.

"Ya wanna do it, Hank?"

Frost looked at the girl. "No—but I guess I assumed all along that I would."

"Excellent," Abdusalem enthused. "Tonight, I shall make many telephone calls, make many arrangements for what must be done, do what I can for the security. Tomorrow we leave for Egypt. There is a safe house where you and the young woman can stay. Then—"

"Then," Frost interrupted, "I go get myself killed. Wonderful." He stubbed out his cigarette and belted away more of his scotch.

Chapter Twenty

The house might have been safe, Frost thought, but it wasn't terribly pleasant. It wasn't far from the city of Cairo itself, in a suburb, he supposed, if suburb were the proper term. The house was really an apartment, not spacious and with windows that didn't open. The windows were constructed of bullet-proof glass with armored shutters that could be closed over them from the inside.

There was air conditioning, a television set, a well stocked refrigerator, a stove and a collection of magazines that ran from the most recent issues of some of the newsmagazines to antique issues of science magazines. Frost supposed the safe house reflected the interests of the people who lived there from time to time.

With Louise Canaretti, Shariff Abdusalem had brought Frost to the apartment and told him he would return that evening to discuss strategy for the next day and report any progress

167

made toward finding the potential assassins. That meant that for the entire day, Frost and the girl would be—essentially—prisoners in the apartment. They could not go out, for if Frost were recognized he would be arrested. According to Abdusalem, Foudani had somehow obtained photos of Frost and of Louise Canaretti and had circulated them to every police establishment in the Moslem world.

Frost turned on the television set out of boredom—then shut it off out of bafflement. He couldn't understand a single word anyone was saying on the broadcast. The set—whether it was a problem of the set itself or due to the fact that perhaps there was only one station—received only one station. Everything else was static.

Frost paced the apartment floor, watching with a combination of amusement and amazement as Louise Canaretti puttered around the kitchen. Finally, he walked into the small room, leaned against the refrigerator and started to ask what she was doing. Before he could open his mouth, she walked over to the refrigerator and told him unceremoniously, "Move it, Hank."

He moved, she got something from the big white box and closed the door. Then she turned her back on him, going over to the counter.

Shrugging, Frost walked up behind her, saying, "I give—what are you doing?"

"I'm makin' us lunch—what's it look like?"

"Ha," Frost laughed. "What's it look—"

"Yeah?" She turned around to face him, her jaw set, a butcher knife clenched in her fist.

"I was only kidding—honest!"

"Yeah," she smiled. "Me too."

"Come here a minute," Frost told her.

"The food'll burn . . ."

"Turn it off."

"Then it'll spoil . . ."

"Then it'll spoil—turn it off."

"Why? I turn you on, so I should turn it off?"

"Something like that," Frost told her.

"Nothin' on TV, huh?"

"Shut up." Frost pulled her into his arms, caught her blonde hair at the nape of her neck and cocked her head back.

"You gonna scalp me or kiss me?" the girl wisecracked.

"What do you think?" But he didn't wait for her to answer. He crushed his mouth down on hers, feeling her left hand fumbling behind her. He looked—she shut off the stove.

They walked together into the small bedroom, the girl pulling the spread off the bed and onto the floor. Frost started to remove his shirt, the girl coming up to him, undoing the buttons, then reaching down and opening the buckle on his belt. She stepped back, her eyes riveted to him as she undid the buttons on her own shirt, then reached around behind her, undoing the attachment for the little white bra she wore.

"It amazes me," Frost told her, "how fast women can do that."

"Practice," she murmured.

"Look, I could tell you stories . . ."

"That'd curl my hair, right? But if I wanted curly hair, I could go to the beauty shop."

"How come they never have ugly shops?"

"Got me," the girl said, thoughtfully, unbuttoning the top of her jeans, then pulling down the zipper. She hooked her thumbs inside the waist of her pants and pushed down, both the jeans and the panties underneath dropping down to her ankles. She kicked out of the sandals she wore and stepped out of her clothes.

Frost pulled off the rest of his clothes and walked the few steps toward her.

"Now what, Hank?"

"We could always play canasta," he smiled.

"Yeah, we could but . . ." The girl hooked her arms around his neck, Frost's hands on her waist. He pulled her close against him and kissed her. After standing there for Frost didn't know how long, the two of them, almost as of one mind, sat down on the bed beside them, the girl leaning back, Frost leaning over her, kissing her, his hands exploring the smallish breasts, the flat stomach, the warmth between her legs.

He felt her hands on him, shifted his weight up and forward and whispered, "I bet you like to lead when you dance, too."

"Yeah, kind of," she admitted, laughing.

Frost pushed hard against her, his body between her thighs, her hands still on him.

170

Finally, he whispered to her, "It feels good—so lead already." Her hands moved very fast then and Frost let out a long breath, closing his good eye for an instant. He decided he'd only go part-way with her—he wouldn't let her lead when they danced.

Chapter Twenty-One

He could always use an extra pair of shoes,
Frost decided. Abdusalem had gotten clothes for
both Frost and the girl, to outfit them as tourists. Part of Frost's new wardrobe was a pair of
white loafers. The size was right. He'd never
gone in for white shoes, but he wasn't about to
look a gift horse in the mouth.

He stood up, looking at himself in the mirror.
White shoes, blue and white seersucker trousers
and a white knit sport shirt with a funny looking
little reptile over the pocket. The .35mm camera
was only a loan, he understood, as he hung it
around his neck. No eyepatch, Abdusalem had
provided a pair of large lensed aviator style sunglasses.

Frost put these on as well, then looked at
himself in the mirror again. "Yuck," he remarked to his image, then walked out through
the bedroom door. Louise Canaretti was already
dressed, sitting there in the living room, talking

animatedly with Shariff Abdusalem. She wore a yellow dress, a sun dress Frost decided. On the floor next to her bare feet was a pair of sandals and on the coffee table beside a straw handbag was a big, floppy straw hat. She'd tried it on when Abdusalem had sent the clothes over and pronounced, "Hey—lookee. We're goin' to a garden party!"

Frost looked at Shariff Abdusalem. "Now what?"

"The Valley of the Kings. I will tell you what I have done, some of it now, some as we go by helicopter to the Valley. You have been there, Frost?"

"No, but when I've been in Paris I've never seen the Eiffel Tower, when I've been in New York I've never gone to the Statue of Liberty—you know."

They drove in what appeared to be a private car through the outskirts of Cairo. A military helicopter waited in an open field for them. Frost was amused watching the girl trying to hold down her dress as the wind of the rotor blades seemingly did all it could to make the garment defy gravity. It would be a long ride, Frost knew from the start, and he settled back, watching the geography so intertwined with history unfolding below them. Abdusalem was silent, and Louise Canaretti, for a moment betraying her education, seemed in awe of the land.

There had been an encyclopedia and several history books in English left in the apartment and Frost, early that morning before Abdusalem had arrived or Louie had awakened, had tried to refresh his memory on names studied so long ago. The Valley of the Kings was also known as Biban Al-Muluk—that determined him to keep mentally referring to it by the simpler name, Valley of the Kings. And the name was quite literal in its meaning. It was the site of some sixty tombs, and there were possibly more that lay undiscovered. It was there that the tomb of the boy king, Tut, had been discovered. Tut's was the only one of the tombs unearthed, Frost imagined, that had been essentially untouched by grave robbers. The thought amused him. The elaborate secrecy of the Egyptian priests had been to no avail—most of the tombs had been robbed well within the confines of the historical epoch in which they were constructed. For a period of approximately five centuries beginning in about fifteen hundred B.C., the kings and their most valued possessions had been placed there. The possessions had been secreted with them to aid them in the afterlife to which the ancient Egyptian religion had been so committed.

Frost wondered if any of the kings had made it. Now, rather than the deeds which had distinguished the royalty of the Nile in life, the modern preoccupation closely paralleled the preoccupation with death—the tombs. The modern Egyptian President, Abdusalem had told Frost earlier, had purposely determined on the site of the Temple at Luxor as the site for his address. The temple was known the world over for its magnificent collonades, and a pilot project aimed at counteracting the effects of ages on the structure was getting underway there. Both the address and the temple restoration were intrinsically tied to one another. The point of the address was to emphasize the history of Egypt and its importance in both the ancient and modern worlds.

The helicopter closely followed the course of the Nile itself, south from Cairo and paralleling As-Sahra Ash-Sharqiyah—the Eastern Desert toward what had been called Upper Egypt. Frost remembered that was why the throne of Egypt had often been referred to as the double crown—Upper and Lower Egypt.

After some time he found himself falling asleep, still not recovered from the days and nights in neighboring Akaran. Somehow the time there seemed almost light years behind him. He remembered Julie Pulman, promising himself once again that if all went well here in Egypt, if he got out alive, he would find a way of getting Sheik Ali Hassan Foudani—killing him for what he had done to the Pulman woman.

Frost opened his eye, Louise Canaretti shaking his arm, shouting to him, "Hank—we're almost there." He yawned, nodded, rubbing his eye awake, wishing he could smoke. It was time to exchange the eyepatch for the sunglasses again and he did that, then again stared below them—amazed. Ahead loomed the Temple of

175

Luxor. He realized then that all the pictures he had seen of it over the years, the times he had seen it used as a background in films—none of that had captured the magnificence.

"We will be landing soon," Abdusalem noted to Frost.

Frost merely nodded—he knew enough about himself to know when there was nothing to say.

Chapter Twenty-Two

The speech, Frost decided, was a handy excuse. People everywhere were the same. Since a large crowd was assembled, there were merchants loudly hawking their wares, there was music, there was food. As Frost, Louie and Abdusalem walked along under the hot sun, Abdusalem almost had to shout to make himself heard.

"There—the speaker's platform. It will be filled shortly."

"It looked just like—" the girl began.

"Yeah," Frost commented, staring at the podium there, "even down to the bullet-proof plexiglass shield there. This is it all right—what they were training for."

"Yes, but as yet there is still nothing definite, no way that I can contact the President's body-guard team and have the speech cancelled, deferred, even have the podium moved out of the way—nothing."

"Nothing on those Nazis?" Frost asked, jostling past a fat man festooned with cheap wristwatches, then lighting a cigarette for himself. He studied the package—behind the Camel was the familiar Pyramid—the thought amused him.

"No one meeting the descriptions either of you provided," Abdusalem half shouted, "has been seen entering the country. But of course the desert is vast, and it is a simple enough matter for someone who knows how to enter Egypt illegally. Even if something does happen, I want you to be aware of the fact that there is no certainty we will be able to link Sheik Ali Hassan Foudani to it. These men he has engaged, as you say, are desperate—that is most certain. Perhaps they will not divulge information if apprehended, perhaps if arrest seems imminent they will take their own lives. Who can say?"

"Wonderful," Frost muttered.

Suddenly Frost wheeled, the girl beside him, holding his arm, digging her nails into his bare flesh.

"What the—" Frost asked.

"It's him—over there," the Canaretti girl nearly whispered.

"Him who?"

"Who is it?" Abdusalem asked.

"One of the Nazis—the young one. I saw him and the other one with Foudani just before one of the harem guards caught me and whipped me. He thought I was just being disobedient. He

178

didn't know I'd been listening."

"Where?" Frost pushed past her, staring out into the crowd.

"I just saw his face for a second—going off that way, I think." She pointed toward the temple itself and the high columns.

In an instant, Abdusalem was beside Frost. He looked at Frost, saying, "I am convinced. The marks on your arms from the girl's fingernails a moment ago—they ring true. Here," and Abdusalem reached under his coat, then looking from side to side to make sure they were undetected, handed Frost a revolver. Frost glanced at it, then stuffed it under his shirt—on quick inspection it looked like an old Colt. "And here," Abdusalem added, reaching from his coat pocket and giving Frost a handful of loose cartridges.

"You have seen the Nazi before," Abdusalem rasped, his face close to Frost's face. "I will take the woman with me. I will go toward the platform and we will search the crowd, you go toward the temple. If you need help, stop a policeman and use my name. My brother is with the Cairo force and involved with the special security here—most of his men know me."

"Super," Frost nodded, then turned to the girl. "Hey—don't try anything heroic. I don't want your father after me too, huh?"

The girl leaned up and kissed him lightly, quickly. "I'll be waitin' for ya when this is over, Hank."

"Is that a threat?" he smiled, then squeezed

her hand, starting off into the crowd and toward the temple. He glanced behind him once, and Abdusalem and the girl were already lost among the tourists and burnoose-clad natives. After several minutes of pushing and jostling, Frost reached the temple itself, the crowd vastly thinner here. He stopped beside a massive statue—obviously of a king. He vaguely remembered the name Ramses II and tried to look for something that would confirm it—he laughed at himself. "Too bad I flunked hieroglyphics," he murmured. Seeing no one nearby, he took the revolver from under his shirt. It was clearly an old Colt Official Police, the barrel roughly five inches long. Pachmayr grips were on it, and—he checked the cylinder—someone had clearly reamed out the .38 Special chambers to accept the slightly longer .357 Magnum round. He decided the gun would kick hard, but it seemed mechanically sound. It had been refinished—it looked to have been Metalifed like his own Browning High Power sitting back in the States now. He remembered Abdusalem's interest in the Browning when they had met years earlier. Frost wondered if somehow the Egyptian agent had gotten the gun into the States and refinished there. He shrugged, stuffing the revolver back under his shirt.

His back to the statue—he decided it was definitely Ramses II—Frost stared back along the route over which he had come. There was the speaker platform—he stopped. Suddenly, the remembered image of the rehearsal arena in the desert valley days earlier flashed into his mind, and he knew he was in the middle of it. The platform, behind it a rock or stone facade, then the clear space between the platform and the spectator area—it was locked with sawhorse barricades now, but had been flagged off back there in the desert.

Frost turned around, looking back along the columns and at the far end from where he now stood—perhaps three hundred yards away. There was a series of lower, different-shaped columns, and spanning these was a flat structure forming a walkway. Suddenly, the whole thing fell into order. He remembered the peculiar wooden scaffolding, the two fatigue-clad men coming down from it, one with a sniper rifle, the other with a submachine gun. Frost stared at the flat area above the far columns, then back toward the speaker's platform. It would be a thousand yards, but there were rifle-scope combinations that in the hands of a good marksman could make accurate hits to twice that distance. Frost had no delusions that the man chosen to make the hit—as Louise Canaretti would have called it—was not a good shot.

He stared back toward the far columns again. He thought, but wasn't sure, that he saw the glint of something catching the sun. It wouldn't have been a riflescope—the optics would have been coated against that. Perhaps a pair of sunglasses, or perhaps the man was nervous and decided to smoke a cigarette, not thinking about the possible reflective qualities of the lighter.

Frost looked back toward the speaker's platform. There was a uniformed police officer about twenty-five yards from him, not looking at him but staring at the speaker's platform. From the distance, Frost could see the platform starting to fill. A tall, dignified, rather dark-skinned man wearing an ordinary-looking business suit was standing in the midst of various high ranking military personnel. It was the Egyptian President. Glancing to where the sport shirt covered the borrowed gun, Frost started quickly toward the policeman, not running in order to avoid attracting any attention if possible from the would-be assassins. The last thing he wanted was to speed them up.

He stopped beside the policeman, tapping him on the arm.

"May I help you sir?" the young officer answered in nearly perfect English.

"Do you know Shariff Abdusalem of the Secret Service—his brother is on the Cairo Police Department?"

The police officer's eye muscles tensed, then he nodded soberly, seeming to draw himself to attention. "I'm working with Shariff," Frost said. "Tell him that I've located the spot where they will act from—over there. Tell him to get his men and to do something about the

182

President—hurry!"

The young officer started to say something, but Frost was already walking away, saying over his shoulder, "No time for explanations—just do it."

Frost was staring toward the far end of the collonades, looking again for some sign of the assassins. He glanced behind him, seeing the policeman moving quickly through the crowd toward the speaker's platform. No one else in sight, Frost reached under his shirt, pulling back on the Colt's cylinder release catch, giving the cylinder a spin and closing it carefully, the Official Police revolver locked in his right fist. He started to run a little—at the distance, if they spotted him, they would have no choice but to shoot or make some other attempt for him. It could blow their entire act and Frost was counting on that.

He'd long ago decided, he reflected, running, glancing along the rows of stone columns with their picture writing looming skyward, that there were some things and some people important enough to die for. The President of Egypt was one of these—it was hard to think of a man in the modern world who more aptly deserved the title "statesman"—and if Ali Hassan Foudani and his Nazi collaborators were successful in pinning an assassination on the Israelis it could indeed start World War III.

Frost's right fist flexed on the black checkered rubber Pachmayr grips on the Colt O.P., the

183

five-inch .38 reamed into a .357 Magnum moving as his body moved, his elbow locked against his side.

There was a vastly smaller stone structure immediately to Frost's right as he neared the span across the columns at the far end of the collonade. It was the thing called a sixth sense again, that and only that that alerted him. Perhaps he'd heard something, perhaps seen the flicker of a shadow across the bright ground. Frost wheeled to his right, the Colt double-actioning in his right fist, the lightweight gun belching thunder and flame, the roar deafening as it reverberated in the stone structure. A burnoose-clad man, massive of build, was wielding a sword like those used by Foudani's palace guards, jumping for him.

As the wrestler-sized man crumpled, the center of his forehead split wide by the .357 158-grain semi-jacketed soft point, Frost wheeled left, firing again—the gun definitely shot a little high. He missed as a second man, dressed and armed identically to the first, came for him. The sword crashed down, Frost sidestepping, the blade whistling through the air, his left hand suddenly consumed with pain, pain almost like he had never known. Despite himself, despite the urgency to react, he looked to his hand—it seemed that one entire layer of skin across the back of his hand had been razor-bladed away, the hand covered with blood, the pain unbearable.

But he had to bear it. The seersucker pants already blood drenched, Frost tripped on a piece of rocky debris, stumbling back, catching himself on the bad hand, the pain almost making him go faint. He squeezed the trigger on the Colt O.P. again, holding low. As the man with the sword swung down toward him, the sword stopped in mid-air, the man spinning around. Frost fired again, the hit impacting in the spine, where the neck joined the back. The Arab fell away from Frost—dead.

Frost got to his knees, the gun, three rounds gone, in his right fist. He looked back along the collonade, expecting to see policemen streaming toward him. There were none. There was a loud shout and cheering. He realized why. The President was getting an ovation from the crowd—Frost didn't want the man's popularity with his people to cause his death.

Frost pushed himself to his feet, roughly snatching a burnoose from the head of one of the dead men, balling the gritty looking yards of cloth around his left hand.

It somehow felt better that he couldn't see it. He looked to the bandaged hand again after a second—the burnoose was crimson. Frost's head reeling, he knew it wouldn't be long before the loss of blood caused him to lose consciousness. He started forward, half staggering along the collonade, the cylinder of the O.P. open and the gun clutched between his bandaged hand and his abdomen as he plucked the empties out, identifying them by the perforated primers. He loaded three fresh rounds in place and closed the cylinder, the gun in his right fist again.

"Gotta reach that walkway," he mumbled to himself.

It was no sixth sense, this time. Frost wheeled left, hearing the once-heard-never-forgotten sound of a bolt working open on a submachine gun. It was the younger of the two Nazis, one of the men from the rehearsal arena, a smallish submachine gun in his hands, something Frost couldn't immediately identify. And there wasn't time—the gunfire making coughing sounds because of a long, awkward-shaped silencer at the muzzle was raking toward him. Frost rolled to the ground, his injured hand taking the impact of his weight, sending shivers of pain through his body. His head ached as he raised it and fired the Colt in his right fist, the gun bucking hard as he double-actioned two shots, then two more.

The Nazi—looking like the blonde-haired archetype of all Nazis, Frost thought abstractedly—looked shocked, his blue eyes wide. The gun was still firing in his hand, but the bullets were smashing into the stone near his feet, chips of stone and dust flying into the air. The Nazi's body reeled as if in a dance, spinning, then stopping, awkwardly, abruptly, falling forward, the gun silent, the man's face slapping hard into the stone inches from where Frost lay.

Frost's head sank to the stone ground—his

186

face was wet with a cold sweat.

He glanced down the collonade—still no one was coming, still the cheering was going on. Frost got his right hand in front of him and under him, the gun scraping on the stone as he moved the hand, then pushed himself up to his knees. He glanced down at the subgun in the right hand of the dead Nazi. The bolt was locked open, the magazine follower partially visible through the ejection port. The gun was empty. He saw no sign of a spare magazine on the shirt-sleeved dead man.

Frost got one foot under him, then pushed himself up, trying to stand, falling forward on his face.

His nose ached—he thought he might have loosened his front teeth—he wasn't sure.

He didn't move for a long moment, his head facing toward the walkway across the end columns. He closed his eye, squeezing it tight, then opened it. On the top of the columns, on the walkway, at the approximate center, he could see something—either a piece of pipe or a rifle barrel. He didn't bother guessing which. Frost got onto his back, rolling, inching across the rough stone beneath him, finally getting his back against one of the columns, pushing himself up, climbing awkwardly to his feet.

But he was standing. Frost shook his head to clear it, then at the near end of the columns traversing the end of the colonnade he saw a wooden scaffolding—again the memory of the rehearsal arena flashed into his mind for an instant. It was exactly the same. Frost lurched away from the column, toward the scaffolding.

He stopped at the base of the wooden structure—the walkway above was approximately thirty feet over him. The cheering was still going on, no help coming down the collonade.

Frost reached out with his right hand for the wooden structure, grasping the first rung, staring up. "Can't," he told himself. Then, "Gotta." He jammed the Colt O.P. into his trouser band, not bothering to hide it under his shirt—the blood-drenched burnoose wrapped around his left fist would attract more attention than any gun.

Frost's left hand useless, he hooked the wrist over the next rung up and started to drag his feet after him. The rungs were close together, doubling the number of steps he had to take, but at least making the move from one rung to the other easier.

The cheering was starting to slow—the speech would be beginning. That had to be what Foudani and the Nazi's assassins were waiting for. When the President would be moving, waving to the crowd, the chance of a miss was greater. Stationary behind the rostrum, despite the bullet-resistant glass, he'd be a better target. Frost glanced up again—from the angle where the snipers would shoot, the bullet wouldn't need to penetrate the small shield over the podium; the bullet would be travelling downward. In his mind's eye, Frost could see the rifle, coated a dull, matte black or green, the scope locked in its mounts, the lenses coated. On the buttstock would be an index card or a piece of paper, taped there, giving bullet drop figures for various yardages.

He was halfway up the ladder. The thought crossed his mind to reach for the gun, to fire into the air, attract attention. But if he did, there would be no hope of reloading—he had only two rounds in the cylinder as it was. Apparently the snipers hadn't heard the gunfire, the crowd noise obscuring it for them as it had for the police.

There was no choice, Frost decided, but to get topside, then open up and kill the sniper. He remembered the arena again—in his mind the picture flashed of two men dressed as Israeli commandoes, one of them holding a sub-machine gun, a backup man to guard the sniper in just such an event as Frost was about to create. Self-preservation told him to go for the man with the submachine gun, but in that split second when he didn't shoot the sniper, the sniper would shoot the President.

Frost stopped a moment, nearly overcome with fatigue, exhaustion. He wondered how many names there were for it. He thought about Bess—if he died they'd never be together. But then he thought about Julie Pulman. If he died without getting Foudani for her, at least he'd ruin Foudani's plans for power, perhaps bring

189

about his eventual undoing.

Bess would understand, Frost decided.

He started up the ladder again, the vision in his right eye blurring for a moment as pain stabbed through his head—he was good for about another two minutes, he decided. Then he'd collapse from loss of blood or shock.

He stopped on the ladder once again, his head just below the walkway. Hooking his left wrist over the top rung, the pain almost unbearable, he drew his feet up, his right fist curling around the butt of the Colt Official Police revolver.

There was a loudspeaker going, he suddenly realized. He could hear the Egyptian President speaking—he wished he could understand the language. He wondered what the famous man was saying.

Frost shoved his gunhand and his head up over the edge.

Something made the man with the Uzi wheel toward him. Frost fired the Colt, once.

The sniper, an exotic-looking assault rifle with a long-tubed scope held to his cheek, lurched upward from the rock slab, half rolling, the gun discharging as the man toppled forward and off the walkway over the arches. There was no scream. Frost had expected none. The man was dead, Frost's slug impacting into the back of the head.

Frost tried to swing the muzzle of the revolver on line with the man with the Uzi, but the submachine gun was already chattering. Above the gunfire Frost heard the man crouched behind the gunman almost screaming—it was the second Nazi.

Frost felt something tearing into the left side of his neck and his left shoulder. But the revolver was finally on line and Frost fired. The counterfeit Israeli commando rose to his full height, then toppled backward, over the side of the walkway.

Frost tried to move, but his left arm was stuck, stuck in the top rung of the ladder. His vision was blurred. He tried to move the revolver, but then he realized it had fallen from his hand and he didn't know where it was. It was empty anyway.

Frost looked across the walkway. He could see the older Nazi, an automatic pistol in his hand, the man walking slowly across the walkway, toward him. He could hear the man, his voice shrieking. It wasn't English—Frost supposed absently that it was German.

Frost tried shouting back, to tell the man that even though he was alive and he—Frost— nearly dead, that the Nazi had lost. The Nazis would always lose, he wanted to say. And Foudani had lost, too. Frost tried saying that, heard himself talking but didn't think the words were coming out straight.

Frost looked straight up, the sun blinding him, then the shadow of the old Nazi obscuring the sun. Frost's right eye cleared. He could see the muzzle of the gun in the Nazi's hand—a 9mm, he decided from the apparent diameter of the muzzle. He wondered what kind of pistol it was, telling himself inside that it didn't matter—he was already next to dead.

Then the Nazi stopped talking, switched to English, saying, "You will die!"

Frost wanted to crack something about stating the obvious, but his tongue wasn't working. The muzzle of the gun was inches from his face. Frost decided not to close his eye. He'd never seen himself die before and didn't want to miss his one and only chance.

He heard the shot—you weren't supposed to hear the shot that killed you, he remembered. Well, he thought, another old wives' tale down the drain. Too bad he couldn't tell anybody.

He could still see the old Nazi, the gun in the man's hand, but then he couldn't see him anymore, found himself staring up into the sun.

Frost heard a voice below him—oh-oh, he thought! A voice from below—"I really blew it." He looked down, not wanting to see what he thought he'd see. But it was Shariff Abdusalem. Was Shariff dead, too? "Naw," he thought, because Louise Canaretti was standing right next to Shariff. Shariff had the little Walther P-38K in his hands, as if he'd just shot it. Frost had wondered where the Egyptian security man had been keeping it.

"Frost—hold on!"

Frost wanted to shout back, "I'm dead—how can I hold on?" But suddenly—he decided he

192

must have moved—there was the terrible pain in his left hand again.

"Hold on, Hank!"

This time the voice belonged to Louise Canaretti. Frost tried shouting back, "What do you think I'm doing?"—but he decided to close his eye and rest instead.

Chapter Twenty-Three

Frost hadn't seen Louise Canaretti for nine weeks. Six of those weeks he'd spent in the hospital, part of it for therapy. His left hand was a little stiff but it was because of the skin graft, not because of the muscles or bones or nerves. He knotted his tie, looking in the mirror. He'd lost some of his suntan in the hospital. After this business in New York, then a few days with Louise, he was planning to go to London. He'd decided that the only thing to do about working out his life and how Bess fit into it was to work it out with her. He had three hundred and fifty thousand dollars now, the everlasting gratitude of a few highly placed people in Egypt and in the Mafia. Life wasn't so bad, he decided.

He finished knotting the black silk knit tie in place and pulled it up, buttoning his collar. "Inflation," he muttered.

"What?"

He looked at Louise on the hotel bed behind

him in the mirror. "I said inflation, Louie. When I first started buying these ties, cost me eight bucks. This last one cost twenty-eight dollars—that's ridiculous."

"Why don't you wear normal ties then?"

He smiled. "I like these, Louie."

He turned away from the mirror, walked across the room to the little wooden valet stand and took his suit jacket from it and tossed the jacket on the easy chair, putting on the blue suit's vest, then buttoning it. He grabbed up the Alessi rig with the Metalifed Browning High Power, slipped it across his shoulders and went back to the mirror to see how it hung. He wondered if the blue shirt made for too much blue with the blue suit. "Naw," he muttered.

"What you gettin' all dressed up for?"

"Got a date with some of your father's guys—kind of a good deed we gotta do."

"You're gonna knock off that schmuck Foudani. I can read, you know. He's here with some U.N. delegation."

"Isn't it something in the syndicate that you're never supposed to tell a woman what you're—"

"That's bullshit," she interrupted. "You didn't come back to the States to see me. You came to kill him."

Frost slipped on his jacket. "I can't argue with the truth, kid—but I am glad to see you. Be here when I get back?"

"You know I will—I'm stupid," she said flatly.

He grabbed his raincoat out of the closet. "You know, I like these old New York hotels. Maybe this time I'll get to spend a few days and see the Statue of Liberty."

"Don't hurt your pretty face, fella," she laughed.

Frost smiled back at her. "Even if I had one, just for you I wouldn't."

He started to the door, then turned, the girl already off the bed, naked, running into his arms. "Be careful. I mean, I decided I don't love you, but you're a heck of a nice Joe and I'd hate ta see ya get wasted out there."

"Thanks," he told her.

"You goin' back to that girl you talked about in the hospital when you were sick?"

"Was her name Bess?"

"Yeah—I think so."

"Then yeah—I think so."

"You and me gonna—"

"If you want to—I mean I did count on seein' you," Frost told her.

The girl took a step back, turned fully around, then laughed, "There ain't much more of me to see, Hank."

"I'll be back in a while," he said finally.

"I'll wait," she told him, then almost jumped toward him, kissing him quickly on the mouth, then going back slowly across the room. She was getting into bed as he closed the door behind him. He took the elevator—he was trying to overcome his inhibitions—and let out

196

a sigh of relief when it stopped in the lobby.

He walked across the blue and white rug, under the chandeliers and through the archways down the atrociously carpeted steps and to the revolving doors leading out onto the street.

He looked to his left, seeing the railroad station and the truck tunnels that ran on both sides of it where it cut off the street.

The car parked at the curb was almost identical to the one Mr. Canaretti had used in Miami. Frost walked toward it, a dark-suited young man nodding to him, sliding into the front passenger seat. Frost climbed in back, leaning back, the car moving soundlessly away from the curb.

He glanced out the window a few times. He decided that navigating New York City traffic was tougher than the fight he'd had at the Valley of the Kings. Someday he would owe a big favor to Shariff Abdusalem. When the Egyptian had killed the Nazi with a not-too-easy pistol shot, he had saved Frost's life. And, it had been Abdusalem who had been the first one up the ladder to get him down—Frost didn't remember that because he'd been unconscious by then, but Louise had told him. Louise . . . weird girl, but nice, Frost thought.

"We change cars here, Mr. Frost," the young man from the front passenger seat said.

Frost nodded, climbing out. They'd driven longer than he'd thought. He recognized Central Park—he'd been there once before. Maybe he'd take in a play with Louie, he thought.

"This way," the man told him. Frost huddled in his raincoat and nodded—it was early and still cool. The back door of the black car a few yards behind where the limo had parked swung open and Frost climbed in. He recognized the man in the back seat, the man Louise's father had told him would accompany him—just in case. No name had been given, none asked for.

"How ya doin' this mornin' Mr. Frost?" the man said.

The face looked Irish, though the coloring was wrong, and the eyes were kind in a strange sort of way.

"Fine, pal—how about you?"

"Terrif—never felt no better. Here you go— you said you like automatics better." The door closed behind Frost. Frost was aware of the younger man climbing into the front seat beside the driver. The Irish-looking man with no name reached into a black briefcase and extracted a worn-looking automatic pistol. "Even got you one close to what you use, Mr. Frost."

Frost went to reach for the gun, then noted the rubber surgical gloves the man wore.

"Here—put these on." The man handed Frost a large paper envelope. Frost opened it, then awkwardly pulled the gloves on. The skin on his left hand was still sensitive and the rubber or whatever it was irritated it.

Frost took the gun then. He almost laughed. It was a late World War II gun, one of the ones

198

produced under the Nazis after the takeover of Belgium. He could see the Nazi markings clearly along with the abundant proofs. It had a tangent sight and the backstrap of the grip was slotted—he assumed for a shoulder stock. "You know," Frost told the man, "I hope you don't own the stock—it'd make this illegal."

"I'll throw it away soon as I get home," the man smiled.

Frost checked the magazine, thumbing out each round, then checking the spring pressure under the follower, then reloading it. He slapped the spine of the magazine into the palm of his hand, seating the rounds. He slammed the magazine up the butt and worked the slide, chambering the top round and upping the safety.

Frost looked at the man beside him. There was a pump shotgun in the man's hands, the buttstock sawed away and a hook on the end. He judged the magazine as a standard five rounder, which meant it held only four. The barrel was sawed away an inch in front of it. "I won't stand too close," Frost told the man.

"Good thing," the man smiled. "We're almost there."

Frost looked up, hearing the bolt clicking back on a submachine gun. He glanced over into the front seat. It was a vintage Thompson, the dark-suited young man holding it. "For nostalgia's sake," the man smiled. "But loaded up with armor piercing for the windows."

"Terrific," Frost smiled, asking himself silently, "What am I doing with these guys?"

The young man with the "chopper" was talking now over a CB radio. Frost couldn't make it out clearly enough to get the words coming back. Frost looked out the window—he decided Central Park was really lovely in early autumn.

"That's them up ahead," the young man with the submachine gun remarked.

Frost leaned forward—there was a utility truck parked in the two lane street, near one of the bridges, blocking one lane. A short distance behind it—just visible—was a work crew with some kind of equipment blocking off a manhole.

"We got the Sheik comin'," the man with the Thompson said.

Frost decided to lean back and ride with it, wondering if he'd get the chance to say anything to Sheik Ali Hassan Foudani before he killed the man.

Frost could see an elaborate limousine coming toward them as his car passed the utility truck and the work crew. The limousine made Canaretti's custom car look like an economy import. The limousine passed the car Frost was in, the driver of Frost's car hitting the brakes hard, cutting the wheel into a sharp left, the car bootlegging into a one hundred-eighty degree turn, then the motor roaring as it started after the limousine.

200

Frost felt the safety on the pistol in his right hand. The limo was starting to speed up, going under the bridge. Frost could see the utility crew jumping into the bushes, the utility truck pulling out, blocking the street, the limo lurching, stopping, then starting a fast reverse.

"Hold on tight, guys," the wheel man shouted to Frost and the others, cutting the wheel in another hard left, the car fishtailing as the limo reversed toward it.

Frost almost hit the floor, the impact of the limo hard against the rear end of the car.

Then it was happening. Frost started out his side door, the Irish-looking man with the shotgun starting out on the opposite side. Frost remembered the drill—he kept below the roof line of the cars.

The Thompson was already opening up, the glass on the driver's side of the limo shattering under the impact of the armor-piercing rounds. The off-side passenger door opened, and a man with a small submachine gun in his right hand surfaced over the roof line.

There was a loud blast—the shotgun—then another, the bodyguard with the submachine gun vanishing below the roof line, the face shot away.

Frost still held back. The Thompson chattered into the locking mechanism of the driver's side passenger door and Frost heard a shout from Canaretti's gunman, "Go for it!"

Frost reached for the door handle, pulled hard

and dropped—there was a fusillade of small arms fire, then the roar of the shotgun.

Frost heard the voice of the Irish-looking man. "Now!"

Frost pushed himself up, looking into the back seat of the limousine. There were clothes covered with the bloodstains of other men. And there was a white burnoose—bloodstained, too—half-covering the face that belonged to Sheik Ali Hassan Foudani.

Frost shoved the 9mm pistol ahead of him, the muzzle inches from the Sheik's face.

"Do it!" Frost heard the man with the Thompson shouting.

Foudani looked at Frost, saying, "Please—I beg of you!"

Frost looked at Foudani. The Irish-sounding man was shouting again, but Frost wasn't listening. "What did Julie Pulman say? What did she say when you told her you were going to cut out her tongue when she tried to stop you from whipping a young girl? You cut out her tongue, you son of a—" and the roar of the 9mm slug belching from the muzzle of the pistol in the narrow confines of the limousine drowned out the last word, the slug tearing into Foudani's open mouth—the tongue. The Sheik's head rocked back, the eyes open and bulging, blood spurting from the front of the face.

Frost pulled back out of the car. The Irish-sounding man was shouting, "Let's get out of here—okay?"

"Wonderful," Frost told him, then climbed

back into the rear seat of the black car.

It wasn't wonderful. The day killing some-body became wonderful was the day he'd stop—Frost had promised himself that years back. "But it does feel damned good," he whispered as he leaned back in the seat, staring up at the trees.

Chapter Twenty-Four

Frost stared through the curtains—it was getting light and had been for some time.

Face it, he told himself. It's morning.

The play the previous evening had been interesting—he had never seen a Broadway play before. Dinner had been superb. He looked at Louise Canaretti in the crook of his left arm. They had made love before the play, then again afterward. She was a strange girl, he knew—but he liked her.

In a few more days he'd leave, probably never see her again, not even to pass on the street.

He exhaled hard, easing his elbow out from under her neck, swinging his legs out of bed. He stood up and went to the bathroom, then afterward stared at himself in the mirror. The scars on the left side of his neck and the left shoulder were healing well enough. He shrugged, searching the bedroom for his cigarettes, lighting one, leaning back in the easy chair. He decided he should take a shower, get dressed.

Frost stood up, stretching. At least Foudani was dead. Nothing could bring Julie Pulman back, but Frost had avenged her. He smiled—he had never done anything so earth-shattering before as saving the life of a President. At least that had worked out successfully.

He started for the bathroom, but decided against the shower. He lit another cigarette. Looking around the room, there was nothing to do. "What the—" He stood up, turned on the television set and leaned back. Color television intrigued him—he thought maybe he'd get one someday.

". . . has as yet been no official word from Cairo, nor from Washington. Word was given to the President at approximately—" Frost turned up the volume, sitting back again in his chair, "—that the assassination attempt had taken place." He leaned forward. "And, though it isn't official yet, informed sources indicate that, in fact, the President of Egypt has been killed."

Frost stood up, shut off the television and walked to the window. He pushed back the curtains, threw up the window and shouted outside, "For nothing!"

"What?"

Frost turned around, saw Louise Canaretti sitting bolt upright, her eyes blinking at the light. "It was all for nothing, I said," Frost told her. He closed his eye and sat down on the edge of the bed, the cigarette burning between his fingers, wishing there was a bottle in the room. Whiskey—but somehow he was glad there wasn't.